PERFECT

PERFECT LOVE

5.5 WAYS TO A LASTING RELATIONSHIP

SHUBHA VILAS

First published by Westland Publications Private Limited in 2018
61, 2nd Floor, Silverline Building, Alapakkam Main Road, Maduravoyal, Chennai 600095

Westland and the Westland logo are the trademarks of Westland Publications Private Limited, or its affiliates.

ISBN: 9789387578562

10 9 8 7 6 5 4 3 2 1

Typeset in Arno Pro by SÜRYA, New Delhi
Printed at Thomson Press (India) Ltd.

CONTENTS

AUTHOR'S NOTE

'There is only one happiness in this life: to love and be loved.'

'Marriages are made in heaven.'

These two ideologies are almost always the backbone of love stories with happy endings. But when it comes to real life, the truth is very different. Love is possibly the most painful reality that people face in this world. Often those who love deeply with all their hearts are the ones who are most pained due to unmet expectations.

More movies have been made, more novels have been written on the theme of love than on any other subject. And, amazingly, at least half these movies and novels portray frustrated love and the upheavals it causes in life. The point to ponder over is this: If love is such an overwhelming emotion in human society, then why does it not last? Why is humanity losing faith in the existence of true love? Why are people losing faith in the institution of marriage? These and many such questions surface as soon as one hears the word 'lasting love'.

Given this scenario, this book explores the idea of eternal love, love that withstands the test of time. This is not just a book of fictional love stories. Nor is it a book that gives superficial self-help tips for creating enduring relationships. This is a thought-provoking narrative that presents six attributes of relationships that can make your love story a phenomenon that lasts a lifetime.

Embedded within these six ancient stories are five-and-a-half secrets that will make your new-age love story outlast the clock. Why five and a half, you wonder? For that secret to unfold, you have to wait till the very end! Flipping the pages to the last chapter will only spoil the fun of the learning.

Perfect Love: 5.5 Ways to a Lasting Relationship contains six of the oldest love stories known to mankind. They have been told and retold from time immemorial. Yet they are worth exploring and retelling in the modern context. Some of the greatest treasures of the earth are buried deep in the fossils of time. Only when you dig deep enough do you get rich enough. This book tries to excavate lost lessons from these ancient love stories that have been buried with time. Youngsters may not even recognise most of these stories. Those in their middle-age may know some stories they may have come across in their younger days, but may not remember the finer details that make these stories so enthralling. The older generation will possibly know the details, but will definitely not know the deep wisdom that underlies these stories. This book is a combination of story-telling and life-altering wisdom. As you read the stories, you will realise that each one of them is worth a book in itself.

Derived primarily from the Mahabharata, the Srimad Bhagavat and the Kathasaritsagar, the selected six stories have some nail-biting twists and turns with edge-of-the-chair adventures. A potpourri of multifarious love stories, these six tales will touch your heart, the exploits narrated in them will exhilarate your mind and the wisdom within them will inspire your intellect. All at once!

You may ask that in an era when the institution of marriage itself is being questioned, does it make sense to read a book that talks about love stories of stable marriages from an ancient age? Find out for yourself by delving deep into this book.

All I ask is an open heart and an open mind for the love to flow into your being.

Chapter 1

THE WHEEL OF FORTUNE

'This is a story of magic, intrigue, deceit, speed, revenge, determination, wit, sorrow, joy and, over and above all, it's a story of true love. This is a story that can make you cry and laugh at the same time. This is the story of all stories!'

On hearing their mother speak these words, the golden baby swans gathered around her. They knew that their mother's big belly was filled with stories. That's what their father always told them, at least whenever he needed peace from their incessant chatter. On seeing the eager bunch of listeners gather around, the mother swan carried on with her narrative. 'In fact, I was very much an integral and important part of this story.'

Wow! That fascinated them even more. The story of their mother's adventures! They huddled closer, as if entering into her secrets. With dramatic flair, the mother swan narrated this most intriguing story, fluttering her golden wings with vigour and enthusiasm.

'As much as Nala was handsome, Damayanti was gorgeous, if not more. As intelligent as Nala was, that much if not more was Damayanti witty. As much as Nala was strong, that much if not more was Damayanti determined. As much as Nala was an expert at riding horses, that much if not more did Damayanti ride through every man's mind. As much as Nala was truthful, that much if not more was Damayanti pure. Nala was the king of Nishada country and Damayanti was the princess of Vidarbha country and the daughter of King Bhima. Word of Nala spread throughout the world and word of Damayanti spread through all three worlds.'

'That's where I enter the story!' Now the young ones were glued to their mother's words. She continued dramatically, 'The Nishada kingdom has some of the most serene water bodies. A flock of us golden-winged swans often frolicked in the watery abodes of the kingdom, especially in the palace grounds. As we were enjoying ourselves, unbeknownst to us, King Nala was observing us keenly from a distance. Without realising it, we literally walked into him. Only when we got too close did we notice his presence and we panicked. In the confused hustle bustle that followed, all my friends managed to fly away, while I was caught by the king. Out of great fear of losing my life, I began to speak in the human tongue. When the king saw that I could communicate in his language, he was pleasantly surprised and held on to me even tighter.

'I realised that if I wanted my freedom back and not end up in a fancy cage in the palace, I would need to bargain my way out of the situation. I told him that it could benefit him more if I was free rather than bound. Intrigued by my proposal, he inquired in what way I could profit a king as powerful as him. I cleverly explained that every king is looking for a perfect queen to share his life with. And that I knew exactly the person he deserved. As soon as he heard this, his grip slackened on me. I knew I had hit the mark. I began to describe Damayanti's flawless beauty to him.

As I began to narrate every delicate feature of Damayanti's body and personality, Nala began to sway ecstatically in anticipation of making her his own. By the time I finished, the king was madly in love. Without even seeing her or knowing her, he was determined to have her as his life partner. He knew that love is not at all about looks but is about a match of qualities. As I described the divine qualities of Princess Damayanti, Nala instantly felt that this was the girl he had always wanted to dedicate his life to.'

❁ *Don't just look for compatibility with the one you love but look for connection. Connection is not just about rhyme but also about rhythm. For connection to happen, it's not only the quality of life that has to match but also the speed.*

'I then made a pact with the king. I told him that if he set me free, I could make Damayanti develop an irresistible love for him. The king released me in an instant and off I flew to the courtyard of Princess Damayanti. In a matter of a few minutes, I invoked intense love in the princess's heart for King Nala. She was literally swooning in desperation to meet him. No matter how much I told her about the Nishada king, she wanted to know more. She was so captivated by his good qualities, she was determined that if there was anyone she wanted to spend her life with, it was Nala. Achieving my goal, I flew off.'

Damayanti got lost in thoughts of Nala and, over time, her internal state of mind clearly manifested in her external behaviour. Soon everyone in the palace realised that she was lovesick. Reports were sent to King Bhima, who immediately took action and decided to organise a swayamvara to find his daughter, who had come of age, a suitable partner. He reasoned that if he invited all the kings of the world to this event, the person whom his daughter had set her heart on would surely come to claim her hand.

As the word spread, suitors from across the globe began flocking to Vidarbha. An overwhelming number of kings and nobles came to claim the hand of this one maiden. There was a look of fierce competitiveness in their eyes. They all realised that only one of them would return satisfied from Vidarbha. King Bhima organised luxurious accommodations for each of his royal guests.

As Vidarbha became a beehive of activity, there developed an unnatural emptiness in the court of King Indra, the supremo of the heavens. It was a special court day and he had invited some of the most powerful mortal kings from the earth to participate in an important item of discussion concerning universal affairs. Just when Indra began to wonder why such an important meeting had garnered such sparse attendance, the celestial sage Narada walked in and informed him of the exciting swayamvara event of the beautiful Damayanti, which the kings had prioritised over the dry divine meeting.

❁ *People prioritise adventure over responsibility because they are wired to prioritise excitement over anxiety.*

Just the name 'Damayanti' caused the four most powerful gods, Indra, Agni, Varuna and Yama, to stand up in absolute reverence. Seldom had an earthling caught the gods' attention in such a way, let alone affect them so much. They expressed their thoughts to one another. Indra said, 'Such a beautiful girl should surely be wed to someone in the celestial realms. Surely no one on earth deserves her.' Agreeing completely with Indra's opinion, the four gods set out to bring the unrivalled beauty to the place that she rightfully belonged—the celestial realms.

❁ *The toughest task is to retain the attention of those who are used to attention.*

As the four of them were entering the precincts of Vidarbha, they saw a brilliantly handsome man zipping towards the city gates, riding on a chariot that moved at the speed of mind. Instantly, the gods knew that his presence in the swayamvara posed the greatest challenge to the possibility of their winning Damayanti's hand in marriage. Though they were gods, Nala's beauty, skills and lustre seemed to far exceed theirs. It seemed to them that Nala was Kama personified and was challenging them openly. As they stared, the rapidly moving chariot came to a screeching halt. Nala looked in their direction as if he already knew what was on their minds. Alighting quickly, he reverentially joined his hands together in greeting as he walked towards the four gods. From their unique characteristic features he immediately knew who they were. He was flattered that these powerful universal administrators had chosen to stop him over the thousands of kings and monarchs who were entering the festive city of Vidarbha. Nala stationed himself humbly in front of the gods with palms folded, in all sincerity wanting to serve them. Without even asking for his name, Yama, who possessed a detailed database of every living entity in the world, spoke to him. 'King Nala, we know you to be an excellent leader and an ardent upholder of the truth. We, the gods, seek your help.'

Embarrassed at a request from such exalted personalities, Nala agreed and asked them to command him in any way they pleased. He regretted his words soon after.

'We want you to deliver an important message right now.'

'Tell me!' Nala enthusiastically responded.

'Go to Damayanti and tell her that she should choose one amongst the four of us as her husband.' The words that spilled out of Indra's mouth fell on Nala's head like a thunderbolt.

Nala realised that these gods had tricked him by asking him to commit to an action before revealing the task. He began to stammer, lost for words. 'But… But I have also come here for the same purpose. Moreover, I am intensely in love with the princess. It won't be fair on me if you make me your messenger. How do you expect me to do this?'

❁ *Committing before understanding is like burping before eating. It's a serious sign of indigestion.*

'But a promise is a promise!' Yama proclaimed in his characteristic steely voice of death.

Not willing to succumb to their pressure, Nala tried to find some way out of this dilemma. 'The women's quarters in a palace are always heavily guarded and absolutely unapproachable,' Nala blurted out in a last desperate attempt to wriggle out of this entanglement.

'Don't worry!' spoke Varuna in his watery voice. 'You just need to walk into the palace; we will take care of the rest.' The four gods had naughty grins on their faces. Nala knew that they were capable of almost anything.

With his head reeling in confusion, with not even a chance to express his frustration, Nala entered the city of Vidarbha. Gaining information about the whereabouts of the palace of the princess wasn't difficult. On reaching there, Nala tried to enter through the side wall of the palace, trying to be as discreet as possible. However, as soon as he jumped across the wall, he landed straight in front of a sentry who was on his rounds. Nala froze! Interestingly, the sentry walked on as if Nala didn't even exist. That's when it dawned on him that this is what the gods were referring to when they said that they would take care of the rest. They had made him invisible to the sentries. With no fear of being spotted, Nala walked in confidently into the palace and reached the innermost section. As he was going to step into what seemed to be Damayanti's bedroom, it struck him that this was the first time he was going to gaze upon his beloved. His heart began to palpitate and his hands began to sweat in anticipation of that first glance. At the same time the awkwardness of the moment also registered in his mind. Hesitantly, he stepped into the room.

Surrounded by a bevy of maids was seated the most stunning beauty, appearing like the golden whorls of a lotus flower. Ablaze with an effulgence that Nala had never seen in any mortal woman, Damayanti looked beautiful beyond belief. His eyes seemed locked in her smile. Every little movement of hers seemed like a dance. When she laughed, Nala almost swooned. He tripped and inadvertently displaced a flower vase that was placed on an ornately carved wooden table. Instantly, there was silence in the room. All eyes moved to the door, and then settled on the smashed flower pot. While everyone else seemed confused about what had caused the flower vase to topple, Damayanti's eyes were riveted on Nala. She gaped at him. She couldn't believe what she was seeing. How could this be? How could he be here? Had her madness reached the point of hallucination?

As she pondered in wonder, Nala walked into the room

unfazed, unseen by anyone else but Damayanti. With a wave of her hand she dismissed all her attendants. At no point did her eyes leave Nala's. Without even a single exchange of words, both seemed to know each other, as if they had for ages. Every pore of her body yearned to touch him. Every pore of his body yearned to receive her touch. As she reached out to hold him with shaking hands, Nala withdrew sheepishly, with a jerk. He counselled his mind not to be swayed from his promise to the gods. He decided not to look into her eyes.

❁ *Physical connections are born after prolonged mental connections, just as a butterfly is born after a caterpillar metamorphoses.*

'O princess, I am here on behalf of the gods. Please note that the four invincible gods, Indra, Yama, Varuna and Agni, seek your hand in marriage. I am a mere mortal and an ant in comparison to these immortal celestials. Please make your choice carefully in the swayamvara. I know you are intelligent and will make a choice that is both ethical and will not bring harm to either of us.' On saying this, Nala turned around and made his exit.

Observing Nala's behaviour, Damayanti realised that he was in serious peril. Understanding his predicament, Damayanti did not prevent him from leaving. She realised that in those few words Nala had spoken, he had actually left her a hint. Now she knew exactly what to do.

❁ *Rather than change unchangeable circumstances, learn to change the changeable attitudes that help to deal with those circumstances.*

Feigning innocence, Nala returned to the eagerly waiting gods and narrated his communication with Damayanti truthfully.

On hearing of Damayanti's reaction to Nala and her eagerness to have only Nala as her husband, the gods realised that they would have to resort to mystical aids to win her hand.

Fragrances of all types wafted through the assembly hall of the royal court as thousands of kings, princes, warriors and heroes streamed in. Thousands of voices conversed in the huge assembly hall, harmonising into an incomprehensible buzz. The only subject of every conversation was the gorgeous Damayanti.

A sudden silence fell as soon as the curtain on the far end of the assembly hall slid open. There stood the stunningly pretty princess in all her glory. Holding a garland in her hands, the delicate fairy-like creature began to walk forward towards the thousands of assembled suitors mesmerised by her, eagerly wishing for a single glance or, if more fortunate, a smile. Her eyes danced around the room, looking for the one she was dying to see. Initially, as she began to walk, inspecting the suitors, she took slow strides, so as not to miss her beloved. But as she passed so many men that she had no interest in whatsoever, she realised that she didn't even need to see him to find him. She would be attracted helplessly to his person just by being within the purview of his magnetic presence. Her pace increased as she desperately looked for her love. After passing every single suitor in the assembly hall, she finally arrived at the farthest section of the hall in great anxiety, where a mind-boggling surprise awaited her. She froze, gaping in amazement. The garland in her hand almost dropped. Her head reeled.

Standing in front of her were five Nalas!

Unbelievable. How could there be five people who looked exactly the same in every way? She tried looking more closely at the five clones to see if there was any peculiarity in her Nala that she could differentiate him with. Nothing at all! Every single gesture and movement was synchronised to perfection. It seemed that they were mirror images of each other. By this time she had realised that the four gods that Nala had mentioned to her had morphed into Nala's form to make it impossible for her to recognise the original Nala she loved. This was most definitely a test of her love. She closed her eyes and began to recall all the knowledge she had about the life and characteristics of the gods. In a moment she recollected that gods have five distinct features that differentiate them from humans. Opening her eyes, she inspected the five of them standing in front of her. The theoretical knowledge that she had was useless. These gods had managed to cleverly hide their godliness!

❁ *For people to recognise the godliness in you, they have to see the humanness in you.*

Left with no choice, Damayanti closed her eyes and folded her hands and in her mind began offering prayers to the four gods standing in front of her. 'O great gods, please know that I offered my life and soul to Nala the very moment I heard of him. Once a girl sets her heart on someone, it is impossible for her to think of anyone else as her life partner. I beg the four of you to kindly help me connect with the one person I have set my heart on. I will be eternally obliged to you.'

As soon as she opened her eyes, she saw five distinct characteristics in four of the five men who stood before her. Their eyes did not blink whereas Nala blinked his. Their bodies did not perspire whereas Nala's body was perspiring out of anxiety. Their garlands appeared fresh and wafted celestial fragrance whereas on Nala's garland some flowers were wilting.

Their clothes were shining and dust-free whereas Nala's clothes had become a little dusty. Above all, their feet didn't touch the ground but rather hovered one inch above it, whereas Nala was very much grounded.

❁ *Those who cannot find similarities in spite of distinctions will easily find distinctions in spite of similarities.*

Damayanti instantly placed the garland around Nala's neck and stood shyly by his side glancing up at him in adoration. There was a huge uproar of disappointed contestants in the assembly. But the world didn't matter to Damayanti anymore. She had got her world. Nala's eyes brimmed with love. With a voice drenched in emotion, he spoke to her, 'You have chosen me over the gods! I am so grateful for this honour you have bestowed upon me. I promise you that I will always stand by you no matter what we go through in life. As long as I live, I will be committed to you!'

❁ *The commitment to be grateful in a relationship is the commitment that keeps a relationship.*

Damayanti was touched by Nala's words. Shedding tears of joy, with folded hands she offered her life to Nala. The happy couple turned towards the four gods who had by now assumed their original celestial forms. Touching each of their feet, Nala and Damayanti sought their blessings. The gods were pleased with Nala's attitude and conferred on him two benedictions each. Indra blessed him that whenever he offered a sacrifice, Indra would personally appear to accept the offerings. The king of the heavens also blessed him with an assurance of admission to the heavenly realms in the afterlife. Agni offered him the boon that he would gain mastery over the element of fire and that he would be able to invoke it anywhere, at will. The god of fire also offered him admission to the heavenly abodes. Yama granted him the ability to expertly perceive the subtle tastes in different foods. The god of death also blessed Nala that he would be a monarch of righteousness. Varuna in turn offered him complete command over the water element, which meant he could invoke water anywhere and at any time just by desiring it. The god of water also gifted him with unfading celestial flower garlands.

As soon as the gods ascended back to the heavens, King Bhima declared that the marriage ceremony would take place the next day and invited everyone assembled to participate in the royal wedding. Musical instruments resounded throughout the city at once and a festive atmosphere prevailed. As the four gods returned to their celestial abode, years were passing by on earth. Time behaves differently on earth than in the heavens. What is but a moment in heaven is six months in earthly time. On their way to their heavenly abodes, the gods came across two well-dressed divine personalities rushing towards Vidarbha. Stopping them, the gods asked them the reason for such hurry. Introducing themselves as the personified forms of the Kali Age and the Dwapara Age respectively, they spoke in unison, 'We are going to the swayamvara of Princess Damayanti.' Kali then went on to say how much her beauty had infatuated him. Laughing at their ignorance, the four gods explained how the princess had been married to Nala many years ago and, in fact, by now had two children. They explained that they themselves had gone to win her hand, but she chose the earthly king, Nala, over them. Kali began to boil over in great anger.

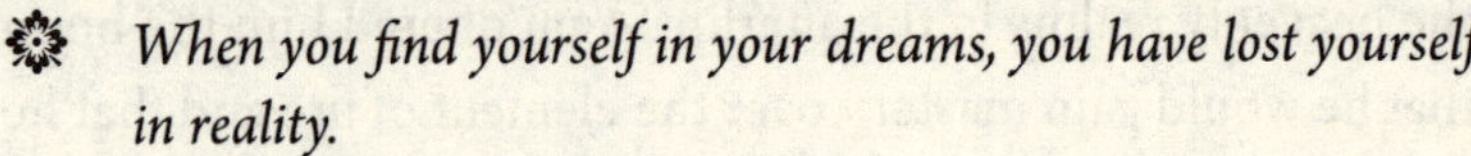

When you find yourself in your dreams, you have lost yourself in reality.

'How dare she choose a mortal human, while rejecting celestials? She has to be severely punished for this audacity,' Kali yelled. Trying to calm this sudden burst of anger, the gods explained to him that she had only married Nala after receiving their approval. They told him that Nala was no less than a god himself in every way. The more they glorified his greatness, the more envious Kali became. As soon as the gods left, Kali began to plot the downfall of King Nala. While beseeching his friend Dwapara for help, Kali became fixed in his determination. He proceeded alone to Nishada to execute his plan after securing a pledge of unconditional help from Dwapara.

Closely monitoring Nala, Kali waited patiently for Nala to make even a small mistake. In order to maximise the peril of this righteous man, Kali decided to wait before playing the masterstroke. The right opportunity arrived after twelve long years when, one day, Nala, in a hurry to return to his duties, forgot to wash his legs after urinating. He went directly to offer his evening prayers. Kali found just the excuse to enter his body and influence his mind.

❁ *The mistake of finding others' mistakes is bigger than the mistake of making that mistake.*

Kali then conveyed a message to Pushkara who was Nala's brother: 'I can help you become the king of Nishada.'

Pushkara's eyes lit up instantly.

'Invite Nala to play a game of dice with you. I will take care of the rest.'

Being thus slyly coaxed by Kali, Pushkara jumped at the idea.

After repeated pushing and prodding, Nala agreed to play a game with his brother. As soon as the game began, Kali began to influence Nala's mind. Being under Kali's influence, Nala felt convinced that he was divinely empowered and would win a huge fortune. Even though he kept losing game after game, he remained certain that he would win back everything he lost in the next game. Each loss made him more determined to win. He became insanely confident of his abilities to regain everything. His friends begged him to stop this madness. His subjects were shocked seeing their king on this losing spree. Damayanti, who was informed of this craziness, wanted to talk to him but the Kali inside him did not allow Nala to agree to her request. The ministers were at their wits' end seeing their king so absorbed in the game. Day and night no longer mattered to Nala anymore. He hadn't eaten or slept for days. His eyes were riveted to the board. The rest of the world didn't exist for him.

✾ *Often confidence is a greater enemy than fear.*
While a person makes the mistake of under-doing in fear, he commits the error of over-doing while confident.

Planning for the inevitable future, Damayanti called for Nala's charioteer, Varshneya. Handing over her son and daughter to him, the queen instructed him to take Nala's fastest horses and take her children to her father's house. Once there, she told the driver that he was free to decide where he would like to stay and work, as his master was not capable of employing him anymore. Varshneya dropped the children off at their grandparents' palace and sought shelter in Ayodhya, becoming the charioteer of King Rituparna.

✾ *An ant that prepares for the winter is better than a human that fears the worst.*

By this time Nala had lost practically everything except the will to play dice. Pushkara taunted him by saying that the only thing Nala could stake now was Damayanti. The mention of her name shook him out of his trance. He removed his ornaments and expensive clothing. Leaving a simple loincloth on, Nala walked out of the kingdom followed by Damayanti, who was dressed in a single cloth. Their subjects had been threatened with dire consequences by Pushkara, the new king, if they helped the losing king and his wife in any way.

Days passed as the couple wandered around in a forest, famished and thirsty. Just as they were giving in to despair, Nala spied two golden-winged birds. Throwing his loincloth over them in an attempt to secure a meal, Nala managed to trap them under the cloth. Running naked towards the trapped birds, Nala felt a bit happier. But his happiness was short-lived. To his dismay, the birds flew away with his cloth. As Nala looked on helplessly, the birds spoke to him mockingly, 'You are the greatest fool on earth. Don't you recognise us? We are the dice that made you lose everything. But we were still unsatisfied, since you possessed that one cloth on your body. Now we are happy, since you are left with nothing.' Letting out a peal of shrill laughter the birds flew away.

A broken Nala turned towards Damayanti and said, 'I am a loser. O my dear, leave me and save yourself from misery. I have lost everything and the whole of creation seems to be plotting against me. Go to Vidarbha and be happy with your family. There is nothing but trouble and humiliation to be found with me.'

❁ *While a winner has to push people away from him, a loser pushes himself away from people.*

Damayanti broke down at his words. Sobbing heavily, she spoke her heart, 'My life revolves around you. I have shared all your joys and it is my right to share your miseries. How can I leave you naked in the middle of a dangerous forest and enjoy the luxuries of a palace? Let us both go to my father's kingdom, where we will be honoured and respected. Isn't my father's palace yours as well?'

Nala explained that it would be beneath his dignity to beg for shelter from her father. Without arguing further, he wrapped himself partially with her garment. Both huddled in a single cloth and hobbled along together. Days passed as they wandered about aimlessly, hunger and thirst their only companions. One day, Damayanti just could not get up any more. Her body was emaciated. She slept, appearing almost lifeless. But Nala, who was still being harassed by Kali from within, could not sleep.

Scenes of all the humiliation he had undergone began to play in his mind. Thoughts of suicide began to emerge. Looking at his beautiful wife lying almost naked on the forest floor covered in dirt, he began to curse himself for his mistakes. He got up and decided to leave her so she could find her own destiny. He convinced himself that as long as she was with him, she would have to suffer. He also felt that her purity would protect her from evil forces and ensure she reached her paternal home. He tore a portion of her garment, draped it around his waist and disappeared into the wilderness.

A few hours later Damayanti got up to discover to her horror that Nala had abandoned her. She was even more shocked on finding that he had torn away half her garment, leaving her partially exposed. Even in this condition, rather than blaming Nala, she only cursed the person who was responsible for bringing them to this plight.

❁ *Forgiveness is the pathway to liberate yourself from the bondage of blaming people who are the instruments of your misery.*

She ran hither and thither, looking for Nala. As she stepped on what looked like a twig, a snake sprang up and coiled around her body. As the snake slithered around her it began to tighten its grip. Damayanti panicked. She began to shriek as loudly as she could. The snake's raised hood was just inches away from her face, its slithering bifurcated tongue was almost touching her nose. The snake opened its mouth widely, exposing its fangs. Just as it was about to lunge forward and strike her, a dagger slashed through the neck of the snake and beheaded it. Its dead body lost its grip and fell like a bundle of ropes at her feet. She could breathe again.

Her saviour appeared from the woods, carrying a bow and arrow. Clearly he was a hunter who had responded to her cries. Seeing her in such a dishevelled condition, he offered to take her home and feed her. As she was gratefully devouring her first meal in days, he was enjoying her ravishing beauty. He began to ask her questions about her life only to hear her sweet voice. He did not pay any heed to what she was saying; he was completely focused on the beauty of her form and voice. She began to feel uncomfortable at his constant staring and intentional flirting. She abruptly stopped eating and got up to leave. The hunter lunged forward to grab her. She turned, right at the opportune moment, and he slipped and fell. 'You wretched fellow! I have never thought of anyone except Nala. You dare touch me just because I am alone and helpless! May the gods strike you dead right now!'

❁ *A selfless act done in the backdrop of selfishness is called duplicity.*

Instantly, the hunter fell down dead. Damayanti left the hunter's place and began to wander through the forest looking for Nala. She had lost all sense of direction. In her wanderings she came across many wild animals but she felt no fear now. She had successfully dealt with the wildest of them all. The human! The rest seemed comparatively harmless. As she walked through the forest, her garment became very dirty and so did her person. In fact, any traces of her beautiful form were completely camouflaged by layers of dust. She appeared to be a madwoman who was scantily dressed.

One day she was sitting on the banks of a river and gazing into its pristine waters, thinking about the twists and turns of her life, when she heard some sounds that were distinctly un-forest like. She ran frantically towards the sound. The scene that met her eyes made her smile and cry simultaneously. A caravan of merchants was travelling through the forest. Suddenly one of them screamed loudly. The caravan halted instantly and everyone looked at the person who had shrieked. There was a young boy trembling in fear and staring at Damayanti with wide open eyes. He had thought she was a witch. The eldest among the merchants, who was also their leader, was a very compassionate man. He walked up to her and spoke gently. She narrated her story to him. Requesting them to help her find her husband, she joined their entourage, which was proceeding to the city of Chedi.

❁ *Just like a rose and a thorn coexist, similarly, compassion and cruelty coexist in life. Whenever you cry from being pricked by a thorn, learn to smile turning towards the rose.*

As evening approached, the merchants decided to camp near a lake and proceed the next morning. In a short while, tents had been erected and soon everyone was fast asleep. In the middle of the night, a group of wild elephants attacked the camp. They were mainly interested in attacking the elephants of the caravan but the noise woke everyone and there was total chaos in the camp. As the elephants ran helter-skelter, they tore down the tents, trampled upon the merchants and toppled the torches, thus setting fire to the camp and the goods. In a matter of fifteen minutes, all that was left of the camp was dead bodies and burnt remnants. The few merchants who had climbed up on trees and managed to save their lives gathered together to inspect their losses.

Confronted with such destruction, they began to curse their luck. One of them said they were suffering because they hadn't worshipped the gods properly. Another said that all this happened due to the ill-omened birds they had encountered during their journey. Yet another pointed out that all this couldn't be the cause as they had undertaken this journey many times in the past. He felt that the only difference this time was the witch travelling with them. She was the cause of their losses. They began to search for Damayanti. But Damayanti had overheard their conversation and managed to escape.

❁ *Most people credit their own accounts with their gains and debit others' accounts for their losses.*

During her escape, she ran into a group of sages who were also on their way to Chedi. On seeing her they immediately understood that there was something extraordinary about her and invited her to travel with them. Soon the group reached the city. The sages went their way leaving Damayanti to her own devices. As she walked along the streets of the city, everyone stared at her.

Partially naked, emaciated, dirty, unkempt and crazy-looking, she evoked varied reactions among the residents. Young boys jeered at her. Men passed lewd comments. Uncaring, she kept walking till she reached the gates of the royal palace. By then a big group had gathered around her. Hearing the commotion outside the palace, the queen appeared on the balcony. Seeing the crowd jeer at a miserable-looking woman, the queen asked a guard to bring her inside. As soon as she glanced at Damayanti, the queen knew that she couldn't be an ordinary person. Though she had the external appearance of a madwoman, her large eyes revealed her royalty. In fact, on a closer look, she resembled the goddess of fortune.

 *Looks deceive, eyes reveal.*
Psychology is the study of the mind through the book of the eye.

Taking Damayanti into her confidence, the queen of Chedi asked her about her story. Damayanti told her the whole story, except for the names of the characters in the story. The queen promised that she would send out people to search for Damayanti's husband and requested her to stay under her protection till then. Damayanti agreed to stay on five conditions. The first was that she would never eat the leftovers from anyone's plate. The second was that she would never wash anyone's feet. The third was that she would never have to converse with any man. The fourth was that if any man tried to seduce her, the queen would have to personally punish him and if he still persisted then he would have to be put to death. The fifth was that she would like to personally interview the search party sent out to find her husband. She made it clear that if any of these terms were not agreeable to the queen, then she wouldn't stay in the palace.

The queen immediately agreed to all her terms and appreciated her boldness. Calling her daughter Sunanda, who was the same age as Damayanti, the queen asked them to befriend one another. Sunanda treated Damayanti with great respect and soon the two became close friends. After days of wandering about in the harsh wilderness, hardly clothed and totally famished, Damayanti was finally in the midst of loving friends.

Meanwhile, Nala's troubles simply magnified every moment and seemed to have no end. Then, one day, as he was venturing deeper into the forest, he heard a very faint voice. Someone seemed to be calling his name. Or was he hallucinating? How could anyone know him in the middle of this dense, godforsaken forest? As he inched closer, the voice got clearer. 'Nala! Please help me!' There again! It was definitely not a human voice. He began to run in the direction of the sound. As he stepped into a remote section of the forest, Nala realised that a raging forest fire was rapidly progressing towards him. The sense of urgency in that alien voice increased as did the frequency of the calls. Nala continued to run in the direction of the voice, understanding well that someone needed to be rescued from the fast-approaching inferno. As soon as he jumped into the small clearing in the forest that was the source of the sound, a ghastly surprise awaited him. He winced and stepped back. An appalling sight met his eyes. A being that was half-human, half-snake was slithering around uncomfortably. When it saw Nala, it joined its hands together and begged for mercy. With tears in its eyes, it requested Nala to pick it up and carry it to a safe place. Understanding that this strange being was immobile, Nala showed compassion. He picked it up and rushed out.

As soon as Nala picked up the creature, it shrunk to the size of a thumb, making it easier for Nala to run. Surprised by the change in size, Nala looked at the creature in admiration. After reaching a safe place, he put the weird creature on a rock and sat next to it. Understanding that it owed him an explanation, the odd being spoke up, 'I am Karkotaka, a naga with magical abilities. After being cursed by Narada Muni whom I tried to deceive, I became immobile. For many years, I have been waiting for you to rescue me. When I pleaded to Narada Muni to reverse the curse, he told me about you. In fact, he gave me an accurate description of the circumstances under which you would come to this forest. The curse would end as soon as you touched me. I am finally free to move and return to my home in Nagaloka. As a token of gratitude, I want to offer you a small bit of help. Pick me up and walk exactly ten steps. On the tenth step, a great fortune awaits you.'

With a ray of hope in his heart, Nala once again picked up Karkotaka and began to walk, counting his steps. As soon as he took the tenth step, the snake bit him hard. Nala shook his arms and the snake dropped to the ground and assumed its original size. Nala was aghast at the wretched creature's ingratitude. The next moment, Nala's skin began to shrivel. His bones began to melt. Unable to retain his balance, Nala collapsed to the ground. Horror of horrors! His skin began to darken and shrivel up. In a matter of minutes, Nala was reduced to a dwarf whose shape was mangled and deformed. His back was hunched and his head bent at the neck. His hips protruded outwards. He was misshapen and had lost all his original beauty. Looking at his hands, which were bent at the wrist, Nala glared angrily at the snake. 'What have you done to me? Why did you do this to me?'

 *Just like medicines that cure you have horrible tastes, in life sometimes good appears as bad. In either case, the result is important and not the perception of the means.*

Though Nala was so greatly disturbed, Karkotaka was totally phlegmatic. With a calm expression on his face, Karkotaka began to explain his disturbing action. 'I deformed you for your own benefit. As long as you remain in your original form, your enemies will look for you and hunt you down. But, more importantly, the poison that I injected into your system will act against the negative energies that have taken possession of your body. You should know that a negative force has entered into your system and taken charge of it. You have become a puppet in his hands. Everything you say and do is totally controlled by him. That explains why you have been behaving so uncharacteristically, to the extent of abandoning your own wife in such a dire state. The venom that I have injected into your system will torment your tormentor. He will soon have no option but to abandon your body and make an exit. But I can assure you that the venom will not harm you at all. I also assure you that from now on you will face no danger from animals with poisonous fangs or from your human enemies with poisonous mindsets.'

As Nala visibly relaxed his tense muscles, Karkotaka continued, 'Allow me to also offer you a piece of advice. You should head towards the city of Ayodhya and meet King Rituparna. Introduce yourself as an expert chariot driver named Bahuka. After seeing your expertise in handling horses, the king will barter his superlative talent with the dice in exchange for being taught horse management. You lost everything because of the dice and you will regain everything by the power of the same dice. Whenever you wish to regain your original form and beauty, just remember me and place these two pieces of cloth on your body.' Handing over two superior looking silken garments to Nala, Karkotaka disappeared.

❁ *When people focus on lamenting upon their misfortune, they miss seeing the fortune cleverly packaged within it.*

Immediately, Nala proceeded towards the kingdom of Ayodhya and very soon arrived at the doorstep of King Rituparna. Since he was so deformed, no one could recognise Nala, including his own chariot driver Varshneya, who was by then in the employ of King Rituparna. Initially, the king was put off by his grisly appearance. But when he heard of his expertise in managing horses, his ability to drive them at breakneck speed and about his extraordinary culinary skills, King Rituparna hired Nala at a salary of ten thousand gold coins and appointed him as the superintendent of the stables. He put his two drivers, Varshneya and Jivala, under his supervision and offered him a respectable residence.

While some stability had come into Nala's life on a physical level, there was intense instability on the mental level. Of course, due to the venom of Karkotaka, the influence of Kali had subsided and that negative influence was much lessened. But what remained was the intense torment of separation from his wife. In his ignorance or in his helplessness he had wronged her so much. He didn't even know if she was still alive. He had been so insensitive in abandoning her, leaving her asleep in a state of partial nudity. But what else could he have done at the time? His mind was so muddled. Of course he hadn't realised that his mind was being manipulated from within by the negative influence of Kali, who had taken residence in his body.

❁ *To pull out a thorn, you prick a needle. To extract poison, you insert venom. Sometimes in life two negative experiences put together cancel each other and give rise to positivity.*

Every evening Nala would sing a song about his unfortunate situation in coded words. Jivala would see him weeping in great agony while singing this song as he poured his emotions into the ode. One day he walked up to Nala to ask him about the cause of his agony and the import of the song that he was singing. Nala avoided disclosing any details about his life but explained the essence of his feelings of separation from his beloved. Unable to help in any way, Jivala left him to his sorrow.

In the meanwhile, King Bhima, Damayanti's father, was deeply concerned about the misfortune that had occurred in the lives of his daughter and son-in-law. Unable to see the pain in the eyes of the children who cried incessantly to be reconnected with their mother any longer, he sent a group of brahmanas to different parts of the world to search for his daughter and son-in-law. They ventured into various directions, determined to find the lost couple. One of the brahmanas named Sudeva, who was a close friend of Damayanti's brother, happened to arrive at the kingdom of Chedi. As he was being offered refreshments at the palace, through pure chance he glanced at Damayanti, who had come into the room for a few seconds. In just one instant, he became almost sure that this was the very Damayanti they were all frantically in search of. When he intercepted her and called her by her name, Damayanti recognised him instantly. The very mention of her parents' and children's condition broke the dam of emotions that she had been holding on to so strongly. Seeing Damayanti weep so bitterly in front of a strange brahmana, Sunanda immediately informed her mother. The queen rushed to the spot and understanding that the brahmana was somehow related to Damayanti's past, began to inquire about her. The brahmana explained in detail the story of Damayanti's woes. After narrating the sad story, the brahmana pointed to a characteristic feature of Damayanti. This was a beautiful lotus-shaped birthmark that was situated between Damayanti's eyebrows. He told the queen that as soon as he saw that mark, he knew it was her, even though she was dressed as a servant and had changed in appearance due to becoming so emaciated.

As soon as the queen of Chedi noticed the auspicious lotus mark, tears began to trickle down her eyes. 'How did I not notice that mark before? By this mark I know that you are the daughter of my sister. Know me to be your aunt. I saw you when you were born in my parent's house in the country of Dasharnas. My father, King Sudaman, got me married to Virabahu, the king of Chedi and your mother to King Bhima, the king of Vidarbha. Damayanti, please know that everything that belongs to me also belongs to you. Please feel free to stay here in royal opulence till you find your husband.'

❁ *Just like birthmarks on your body reveal your identity, your values are birthmarks on the soul that reveal your character.*

Instantly the bond between them changed completely. Damayanti touched her aunt's feet and embraced her lovingly. 'Though you didn't know I was related to you, you took care of me like a daughter. Now that you know our relationship, I am sure you will take much better care of me. But I must return to my paternal home because my children need me now more than ever. If you wish to be of further help to me, kindly arrange for a fast-moving vehicle that will take me to Vidarbha at the earliest.'

So Damayanti was transported to her hometown. King Bhima and his wife were immensely grateful to be reunited with their daughter. They amply rewarded the brahmana and expressed their gratitude in numerous ways. Damayanti ran to her children, who were so excited to see their mother again. Once the happiness of the reunion subsided, Damayanti requested her parents to help her locate Nala. Her father summoned another group of brahmanas in order to commence a new search mission, this time to find his son-in-law.

❁ *Parents are like trees that never change their location. They are always located in the land of selfless, tireless service.*

Before the entourage of brahmanas set out on the search mission, Damayanti addressed them. She told them that they should venture into various cities, towns and villages and shout out a cryptic message that she was about to give them. She told them that they should carefully follow and monitor the activities of anyone who enquires about the message or says anything on hearing it. With these instructions, Damayanti spelled out the message:

'Why would the great gambler tear off half the cloth of his wife and leave her half-naked in the wild forest? Why would a dutiful person neglect his duty? Why would a kind person suddenly become unkind?'

❁ *When you jump to conclusions, you land in the quicksand of confusion.*

Ask rather than bask in conclusions.

As a parting instruction, she warned them never to reveal who had told them to say these words and that they should report the exact words that they hear from anyone, verbatim. She also asked them to gather as much information as possible about the person that answers them. With these clear instructions, the group left Vidarbha and dispersed in various directions. In every city, town and village the brahmanas managed to attract great crowds and when the audience was at its peak, they would repeat Damayanti's message.

After months of wandering, a brahmana named Parnada returned to Vidarbha with an interesting piece of information. He told Damayanti that out of the numerous places he had visited and the thousands of times he had repeated her coded message, there was just one man who gave him an intriguing answer, which he felt was worth communicating to her. Seeing her excitement to hear what he had to say, the brahmana sat down. He told her that he had been to the city of Ayodhya and had conveyed the message in the courtroom of King Rituparna. The king couldn't understand anything and dismissed him from the court. As he was leaving the palace, he was grabbed by the arm and taken aside by a man who had a deformed body.

This man named Bahuka, who happened to be the driver of the king, said, 'When misfortune befalls on a man, his every action is influenced by negative energies. Mistakes made under despair should be forgiven. A person who has been dealt with unkindly, acts unkindly. But behind his unkindness is actually kindness. The great gambler abandoned his wife because with him there would only be great suffering. The greatest protection for a woman is her own inner strength. A husband who doesn't understand the strength of his wife has actually never understood her. Between a man and a woman in distress, it is the woman who takes stable decisions and displays greater tolerance. Understanding the man to be weak and foolish, she should not become angry and upset.'

 *Forgiveness comes between bitterness and betterness. The ability to forgive a mistake is always greater than the rigidity to hold a grudge.*

Tears formed in Damayanti's eyes as she heard these words. Rushing to her mother and revealing in confidence the findings of the brahmana, Damayanti sought a promise of confidentiality from her. She was about to execute a plan to regain her lost husband but she did not want her mother to reveal this plan even to her father. Having secured an oath from her mother, she immediately summoned the brahmana named Sudeva, who had reunited her with her parents. She instructed him to immediately depart to Ayodhya and announce to King Rituparna that Damayanti was going to get remarried and there would be a second swayamvara conducted the very next morning. Since there was no information about the whereabouts of Nala, she had decided to accept another husband.

On hearing this news, King Rituparna immediately developed a keen desire to go and try his luck in obtaining the beautiful Damayanti as his wife. He went up to Bahuka and began to coax him to undertake the long journey in such a short time. When Bahuka, alias Nala, heard that Damayanti was going to remarry, he was flabbergasted. He staggered for a moment, unable to stand. Regaining his balance, Bahuka agreed to the king's request and left to prepare the horses. His heart was unable to accept that his wife was seriously considering remarrying. Just some time back a brahmana had come with that cryptic code from her and he had managed to convey his message. Could she have been so disgusted with his reply that she had decided to abandon him forever? Was she taking revenge? He concluded that no matter what she did, it couldn't be worse than what he had done to her. Another thought simultaneously entered his mind. Maybe she was trying to find some way to help him. The only way to find out was to go there. Completely bewildered by the sudden turn of events, Bahuka yoked the horses to a chariot and stationed it in front of the palace.

✿ *Confusion and clarification are two sides of the same coin. When the side of confusion faces you, turn it around and seek clarification.*

When King Rituparna saw the lean horses Bahuka had chosen for this arduous journey, he lost his confidence. Was this man really as knowledgeable in the science of horses as he claimed? As soon as the king mounted the chariot, the horses' legs wobbled and they collapsed to their knees. The king got off, unsure of Bahuka's expertise with horses. Bahuka reassured the doubting king. Keeping Varshneya at the reins, Bahuka began to coax the horses to run. He murmured a few mystical sounding words into the ears of the horses. In an instant the horses stood up and began to run. The king held on tightly to the chariot mast, expecting the worst. In fact, he closed his eyes expecting a mishap. For a few minutes his eyes remained tightly shut. But when nothing untoward happened, he opened his eyes to behold an unbelievable scene. The chariot was actually flying a few inches above the ground. And in the absence of any kind of friction, it was actually moving at an incredible speed.

❁ *To fly ahead in life, you should have least friction with ground realities.*

Most people are so caught up in sorting out the mess of their ground realities that the friction generated doesn't allow them to take off to their destinations.

Varshneya, who was sitting next to Bahuka, was amazed at his skill. He carefully took note of the style in which he was holding the reins and the style in which he was seated. The way this man was able to manoeuvre horses was possible only by Matali or by Nala. His looks definitely didn't reveal him to be either. But how could anyone else do what he was doing? As Varshneya was lost in his thoughts, the king shouted out, 'Stop the chariot, my upper garment has fallen off!'

Bahuka shouted loudly so the king could hear him through the heavy wind, 'We have already crossed eight miles since the time you dropped the cloth. It is not possible to retrieve it.'

The king was amazed at the speed at which they were travelling. Wanting to buy some time with Bahuka before they reached their destination, the king said something that caught Bahuka's attention—'Just as you have power over horses, I have power over numbers. I can tell you exactly how many leaves and fruits there are on this Vibhitaka tree in a second.'

Bahuka brought the chariot to a screeching halt. 'Impossible! How can anyone tell the exact count of the number of leaves and fruits on a tree?'

'The number of leaves and fruits fallen from the tree exceed the number of leaves and fruits still hanging on the tree by 101. Just these two huge branches of the tree contain five million leaves and 2095 fruits.' The king answered in the blink of an eye.

'How do you expect me to believe that kind of speed of calculation? I won't accept it unless I personally count the leaves and fruits on those two branches. If you are in a hurry to leave, you may take Varshneya and proceed. I will only leave this place after counting.' Bahuka got off the chariot and began earnestly counting the leaves and fruits on the tree manually.

The king smiled and told him, 'Don't worry about counting both branches. Let's just focus on one branch.' He then numbered the leaves and fruits on one branch of the tree. When Bahuka counted, the numbers were bang on. Bahuka was highly impressed with the king's ability. The king told him that god gives each person a special skill that no one else has. By doing that he teaches humans to be interdependent. King Rituparna then suggested that Bahuka teach him his skill in managing horses and, in turn, he would teach Bahuka the science of numbers and mastery over the game of dice.

Bahuka then taught the king the Asvahrdaya mantra that enabled him to control the horses. King Rituparna taught Bahuka the Aksharahrdaya mantra that enabled him to have mastery over numbers and the game of dice. As soon as Bahuka learnt the Aksharahrdaya mantra, he vomited all the poison that was present in his body. At that moment Kali, who had been residing in Bahuka's body all this while and tormenting him intensely, left it and climbed up the Vibhitaka tree. As soon as Kali left his body Bahuka found some respite from his sufferings. King Rituparna and Bahuka continued on their journey to Vidarbha armed with the joy of their new-found knowledge and also in the satisfaction of having shared what they possessed.

✿ *Interdependence is sharing what is most dear to you in exchange for what is most dear to another.*

Dependence is taking, independence is giving, and interdependence is an exchange programme.

The chariot moved at a much greater speed now under Bahuka's aegis. When it finally descended into the kingdom of Vidarbha, it began to produce a sound that resembled the rattle of rain clouds. Immediately, the peacocks in the palace gardens began to cry out. The loud cries of the peacocks filled the city. Damayanti had also heard the rattle of the chariot. She was used to hearing this particular unique sound that only Nala's chariot could produce. She ran at great speed to the terrace of the palace to watch the entrance of her prince charming. She was yearning to see her beloved once again after such a long separation. No matter what she had gone through, nothing had changed her love for Nala. However, when she gazed at the chariot rolling into the precincts of the palace, she felt confused. She recognised Varshneya, and could definitely distinguish King Rituparna. But she failed to see how Bahuka could be Nala, as his appearance had changed in every way possible. Could the rattle of the chariot be because King Rituparna knew the science of Asvahrdaya that Nala was adept at?

✿ *When you look down upon someone, they appear ugly. When you look up at someone, they appear beautiful. But when you look straight at someone, they appear the way they are.*

From the time King Rituparna entered Vidarbha he was lost in thought. He was surprised that there was absolutely no sign of any festivity that indicated that a swayamvara was in progress. The city was absolutely calm and so was the palace. How could such a prestigious event happen without any decoration or the flocking of royal guests? As soon as he stepped into the palace,

King Bhima himself appeared to receive him. Expressing great surprise at the uninformed arrival of King Rituparna, King Bhima welcomed him with utmost respect. Understanding that there had been a miscommunication, King Rituparna concealed his intention of coming to Vidarbha and instead said that he was paying a friendly visit to strengthen his relationship with King Bhima. King Bhima wondered how a powerful king like Rituparna could make a friendly visit totally unprepared. However, both of them decided to drop the subject and not probe further. King Bhima arranged for the royal guest to be taken to his quarters and made sure that he received the best hospitality and care.

Meanwhile, Damayanti sent her maidservant to check on Bahuka. She made her repeat the same message that she had sent through the brahmana. Tears sprung immediately to Bahuka's eyes as he heard Damayanti's message questioning his actions and his unkindness. He repeated what he had told the brahmana, urging her not to be angry at the mistake made during a phase of helplessness and negativity. When Damayanti heard this, she was almost convinced that this was possibly her husband. But she wanted to be doubly sure. She sent her maidservant Keshni to Bahuka again to help him with everything he needed but, at the same time, monitor his every action. She particularly instructed her not to fulfil every request of his immediately but rather delay carrying out his orders and observe his reactions. Damayanti wanted an account of everything human and superhuman that Bahuka did.

❁ *Don't sit angrily in the vehicle of others' mistakes all your life. Learn to get off by forgiving them.*

When others show the courage to admit their mistakes, you should show the courage of forfeiting your anger.

After observing Bahuka closely for hours, Keshni returned with her report. The first thing Keshni said was, 'I have never seen anyone like this. He is extraordinary.' That one statement arrested Damayanti's attention. Keshni continued narrating her observations. 'Whenever he needs water in a vessel, as soon as he glances at the vessel, it fills up. When he holds up a reed of grass and points it towards the sun, it blazes up creating cooking fire. When he holds flowers in his hands and presses them, rather than becoming mangled or withering away, they become more beautiful and fragrant.'

Damayanti wanted to taste something that Bahuka had cooked. Keshni arranged for it. As soon as Damayanti had the first bite, she knew that this had to be Nala. She sent her two children along with Keshni to Bahuka as a final test. As soon as Bahuka saw the two children, he ran towards them, embraced them and began to shed tears. He told Keshni that these children reminded him of his own kids. When Damayanti heard this, she was even more convinced that this had to be Nala. But the last and final confusion was about his looks. How could he change so much?

In order to do away with that confusion, she decided to confront him straightaway. Taking permission from her parents, she asked Bahuka to be brought to her chambers. As soon as Bahuka saw Damayanti, he began to weep. She asked him, 'Who would abandon his wife in the forest partially naked? Who could be cruel-hearted like Nala?'

Bahuka fell on his knees at her feet and began to sob

hysterically. 'I was under the influence of Kali who was controlling me from within. Whatever I did was a big mistake. But I assure you that I had no control over my actions at that point in time. In fact the only positive thought I had was that I totally trusted your purity, which would protect you under every circumstance. I have been living with that wretched Kali in my body for so many months. Fortunately, due to your curses and due to the help of a friend named Karkotaka, Kali was being tortured inside my system and has stopped troubling me. I beseech you to please forgive me for abandoning you in that way.'

❁ *Sometimes insensitivity is the external manifestation of an internal struggle.*

Nala looked up at her and said, 'But after ascertaining that I was alive, why did you decide to marry once again? Are you so disgusted with me for that misdeed?'

Damayanti explained everything that had transpired from the time Nala had abandoned her to her plan to get him back. Hearing about her intelligence and her enterprising nature, Nala was highly impressed. His love and respect for her grew a million-fold. Nala then took out the garments Karkotaka had given him and wore them. Instantly, he was restored to his original beauty. Seeing her husband in his original form, Damayanti ran towards him and embraced him. Pulling their children into their embrace, the loving couple cried tears of joy.

❁ *To tolerate does not mean to hibernate.*

Tolerating does not mean you don't endeavour to restore the original situation.

Of course the next day they gave a proper explanation to King Rituparna, who had been dragged into the situation. The king was kind enough to not take offence. Rather he was grateful to Nala for sharing such valuable knowledge with him. Nala then went to his own kingdom and challenged his evil brother Pushkara to a game of dice once again. This time Nala defeated him thoroughly and regained everything he had lost.

However, Nala decided not to blame his brother completely for his humiliation. He knew that though his brother was the immediate cause, the remote cause was actually Kali. Rather than punish his brother, he embraced him and offered him half the kingdom to rule. After experiencing Nala's kindness, Pushkara was highly ashamed of his conduct. Falling at Nala's feet, he begged forgiveness for all his misdoings. He was a changed man now. All the envy and malice was gone, replaced with love and gratitude.

Nala and Damayanti continued to remain role models of true love, which had stood the greatest tests of time. Their love was the epitome of trust during adversity.

❁ *Every emblem of love is also an emblem of courage to remain together through struggles and differences.*

FORGIVENESS IS KEY

There comes a phase in every relationship that challenges its continuance. A chain of bad behaviour or a series of weaknesses forces you to the limits of your tolerance. For some whose tolerance is lower, a single instance of bad behaviour or a single exhibition of a character flaw can be enough for them to exit the relationship. The human brain has the tendency to remember only feelings that belong to the current circumstances of life and conveniently filter out those from the past. No matter how many beautiful and positive memories you have of a relationship, when you come across bad behaviour or a character flaw in your partner that causes you extreme pain, the past positives are forgotten. The overwhelming love we had for the person melts in the heat of the current pain and leaves behind an ugly puddle of detestation. When a relationship begins, the focus is on the good qualities of the other and, when a relationship ends, the focus has shifted only to the bad qualities.

The story of Nala and Damayanti is a story of the test of the limits of tolerance. However, more than that, it's a story of forgiveness. It's a story of two people who loved each other madly, prioritised each other even over the gods. They saw divine qualities in each other that they couldn't see even in the gods. This story explores the dynamics of what happens when people who have such strong bonds come across weaknesses and flaws in each other. It is also a story in which a relationship reaches the brink of destruction due to the bad behaviour of one partner but is brought back to its original healthy state due to the tolerance and forgiveness of the other partner.

Through this story, where extreme problems caused a rift in a relationship, we are given a chance to think about how our problems cause fractures in our own relationships. We realise how much more tolerance we can practise and our capacity to forgive.

In relationships it is important to appreciate the differences that exist between partners but if you can't appreciate the differences, at least accept them and if you can't even accept them, then learn at least to tolerate them. But everyone's tolerance has a limit. When that limit is crossed, tolerance is converted into contempt. When a relationship reaches that level of contempt, then love morphs into hate. Hate pushes one to diagnose every action of one's partner as selfish or immoral or wrong. In everything they do, no matter what the reason, our critical mind, which is engulfed in hate, only diagnoses their actions as unacceptably inappropriate. The diagnosis manifests itself as conclusive negative words.

When we are hurt, we want to protect ourselves from further damage. The best way for the mind to protect us is to take recourse to the 'flight' or 'fight' mechanism. That is, either withdraw from that person's life or criticise the person so severely that we get an artificial sense of winning the fight. Thus negative words become our weapon. In them reality is magnified manifold. In a heart which is full of contempt, it is impossible to find compassion. Once a relationship reaches the stage of verbally abusive contempt, there is hardly any chance of it reverting to normalcy without expert intervention.

Initially there was extreme love, respect and appreciation between Nala and Damayanti. When there is respect for the other's actions, appreciation is easy. But, at a certain point, when Nala began to show a change in behaviour, Damayanti chose to tolerate it as his weakness. Though Nala lost everything, she accepted him and tolerated his mistakes. But when he took away half of her garment and abandoned her in a semi-nude state in the middle of a dangerous forest, her limit of tolerance was reached. Naturally, there were so many questions in her mind about the reason for his completely unacceptable behaviour. So her mind kept pushing her to develop contempt for him and convert the love she had for him to hate. In fact, her mind was leading her forcefully to verbally abuse Nala for all the troubles and life-threatening dangers she had to undergo. Her mind wanted to project every action of Nala's in the past into this zone of contempt. But Damayanti chose not to listen to her mind.

Tolerate first and forgive next. It's not enough to tolerate the weaknesses of people we love, it's more important to learn to forgive them for it. For every event in your life, there is a fact and a story you have told yourself about the fact. When one goes through negative experiences in life, it becomes very difficult to forgive because we remain stuck to our version of the story, where we are the upright hero and the other person a pervert, a villain. Once we believe in this story, we begin to find ways to hurt the person, to try and make them realise their errors. However, by fanning the flame of anger we are blowing away the lamp of peace.

By not willing to give the person who has hurt us a second chance, we are also denying ourselves a second chance to overcome the pain of being hurt. When we conclude that someone doesn't deserve forgiveness, we are actually saying that we do not deserve peace. By punishing the person we love, we are punishing ourselves. Forgiveness helps you make an attempt to restore what you have lost by not allowing pain to take root.

Damayanti realised that practising contempt would harm her more than anyone else. She realised that Nala had left her to do whatever he needed to do. If she carried hatred in her heart, she would have no peace. Somewhere she felt that hidden beneath Nala's bad behaviour there must surely be an explanation. Her mind kept forcing her to deny that an explanation could exist for such ruthlessly selfish behaviour. But she decided not to be stuck to her version of the story. She decided that until and unless she heard his version, she wouldn't draw any conclusions. So she gave Nala a second chance. Not because he deserved it, but because she deserved peace. She felt that it wouldn't be right to let go of a relationship that was so precious to her due to a lack of explanation of the cause of the bad behaviour. Though in pain, she didn't want the pain to take root in her consciousness. She wanted to offer the benefit of the doubt to Nala, in exchange for the years of wonderful love they had experienced together.

The relationship in which you experience hurt today was your choice yesterday. By honouring that choice, you are reminding yourself to take responsibility for that choice. No matter the good qualities a person may be studded with, there will always be some defective aspects to his or her persona. When you accept a person, you should also learn to accept their flaws as a part of the package. When that person exhibits uncouth behaviour, then you need to think that surely there is something that has triggered that behaviour. Just because you don't know the trigger doesn't mean that the trigger doesn't exist. Once you find the trigger, you will also discover the struggle your partner is going through. The best way to find out about anyone's trigger is to question with compassion.

When you are extremely angry about a person's bad behaviour, it is the best time to recommit to the relationship with compassion. Even a small child lashes out when hurt. Forgiveness helps you break the cycle of hurt. It is extremely important to view life situations from the lens of the person you once loved and now hate. Most people love to act as self-appointed lawyers and build a case against their partners. They create a comprehensive catalogue of wrongs and feel wronged themselves. But instead of listening solely to the cruel critic within us, let's think of giving a chance to the person who has hurt us to give us an explanation for their irrational behaviour. That chance has to be given in a voice of kindness and not in a tone of accusation.

Damayanti was well aware that Nala had been her choice. She had chosen him over four powerful gods and scores of powerful humans. All these years she had basked in the joys of his goodness and for the first time she was experiencing his depraved side. Just because she was uncomfortable with his negative aspect, she didn't want to abrogate responsibility for her original choice. She understood that something had caused him to behave the way he had. Though she wasn't able to clearly ascertain what it was, she didn't want to draw premature conclusions.

When she heard the story from his perspective, she empathised; when she empathised, she forgave; when she forgave, she reconnected; and when she reconnected, she became happy. Her mind was at peace once again, and she could feel the love for him flow back into her heart.

Tolerate first and forgive next. It's not enough to tolerate the weaknesses of people we love; it is more important to learn to forgive them.

Forgiveness comes between bitterness and joy.

Chapter 2

THE GOLDEN LETTER

'I received the best advice on relationships that evening, while sitting on the edge of a cliff at the most important crossroad of my life.' There was a gleam in his eyes as he shared this special memory with the most special person in his life. Subhadra was eager to know what her enigmatic brother had told her husband. 'It was a piece of advice that actually united both of us.' When Arjuna said this with a naughty grin, she got even more excited to know the secret he had concealed from her so far.

'Krishna called it the vocabulary of love! He is the king of this subject and He tried to make me a master of it too. The most amazing thing was that He taught me such a complicated subject in the simplest manner, by narrating an incident from His own life. And He told me that He'd learnt about this vocabulary of love from his wife, Rukmini.' Arjuna fondly recollected the session with his friend Krishna which had changed his life and the way he looked at relationships.

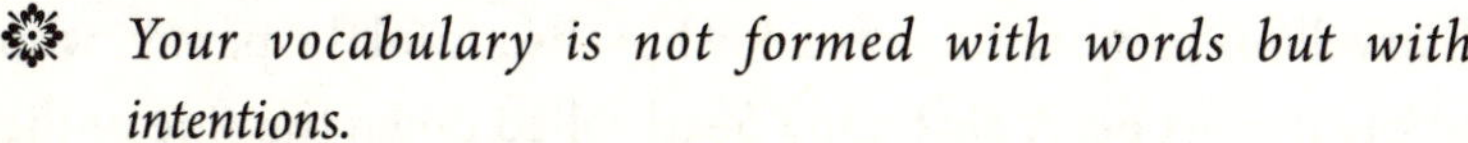

Your vocabulary is not formed with words but with intentions.

When words are woven in an intricate, loving way, they permanently embroider a loving design on the fabric of your heart.

❧

'It's not that the letter arrived at an auspicious moment but rather that I considered the moment the letter arrived to be auspicious.' Krishna pulled out the letter from His belt. It was a letter every child of that era knew about. It was an historical letter and Arjuna felt very fortunate that his friend was actually sharing it with him. In fact, he felt much closer to Krishna at this point in time than ever before. Though their friendship had grown deeper and deeper over the years, clearly this one moment was the defining moment of their friendship. As Krishna rolled open the letter that was made of the most beautifully embroidered soft cloth, Arjuna's eager eyes danced all over, taking in every inch of the beauty of the black silken cloth. He inched closer to Krishna on the rocky stone on which they sat in order to peruse the contents of the letter. Arjuna was like a little child eager to get the first glimpse of a special gift that his mother was unwrapping for him.

❁ *The height of friendship is measured by the depth of the moments spent together.*

Friendship is defined by the number of times your friend redefined you to refine you.

A string of beautifully written words in golden ink shone as brilliantly as the stars in the night sky. Just one glance at the marvellous handwriting revealed how beautiful the person who wrote it must be. A glistening pearl rolled down the side of the cloth. Arjuna realised that the loving memories that had flooded Krishna's mind had emerged from His eyes in the form of that precious tear.

Of the thousands of adventurous things that had happened to Him in his life, Krishna felt that this was the best of them all. Not only because the incidents surrounding the letter were mighty adventurous but also because they were beautifully thrilling. According to Krishna, this letter taught Him the most important element of love, which is heartfelt expression. Though He was the god of love according to the world, He felt that He had learnt the most important aspect of love from that letter. An aspect He eventually mastered to perfection.

❁ *Love is planted by active care, rooted in trust, watered by words, nourished by struggles together, protected by commitment, decorated by fond memories and made to blossom with reciprocation.*

Rukmini had two options before her at the moment. One was to let go. This was the easiest option. An option most girls of her era chose in most cases. The second was to try. An option that could result in a tarnished image or a brutally ugly death. When she thought it through, she realised that she had no real choice. Her heart had already chosen without even consulting her. There was no way she was going to live her whole life with that Shishupala who looked more like a glorified donkey than anything else—happily carrying the burden of self-pride. Rather than dying every moment in the company of that fool, it would be better to die once and for all while trying. But she knew that if what she was trying worked out, she would get to spend the rest of her life in the heavenly presence of the person she loved more than life. A person whom she had never even met so far!

❁ *Living in the company of the wrong person is worse than dying in the company of the right person.*

Vidarbha, her hometown, had always been a beehive of activities. King Bhishmaka, her father, had made the kingdom a flourishing hub for business. His charitable nature had also made it a favourite destination for the devout. Rukmini grew up in an environment that was strewn with influences from various quarters of the world. Growing up in a multicultural environment had brought many blessings to her life and had moulded her into a versatile and talented person. Perhaps the greatest blessing it had brought her was Krishna!

❁ *Exposure to a variety of people, thoughts and cultures is like learning to appreciate all the colours in a set of paints.*

Every so often there would be businessmen coming to sell their wares to the royal household and every other day there would be holy men seeking alms from the princess. As a blessing they would almost always narrate a story of Krishna's latest exploits to Rukmini. The stories would range from His childhood pranks in Vrindavan to His heroic exploits in Mathura, going further to His expert management of Dwaraka. Every story she heard mesmerised her. She would cry, she would laugh, she would dance and she would sing for days together, recalling and reiterating the story. This would continue till she heard the next story, which seemed a million times better than the last one she had heard. She cherished these stories of the person who had become embedded in the core of her heart in the form of ... she had no idea what He looked like. So she stored Him in her heart in the form of words. Every story that she heard, she would render into a beautiful poem and sing it every day. Soon she had a huge collection of poems describing the amazing feats of Krishna. Gradually, these poems morphed into a beautiful shape in her heart. A shape that revealed to her the handsome form of the person she adored so much. Rukmini saw Krishna in a form that probably no one except her could see. In her mind's eye she visualised Krishna as having a form in which every single limb of His body was a quality she adored in Him. Her favourite was His lips, which she envisioned to be the abode of love. When she heard a holy man describe the sound that emanated from Krishna's flute and the effect it had on the world, Rukmini concluded that the lips that could produce such a magical melody had to be full of love.

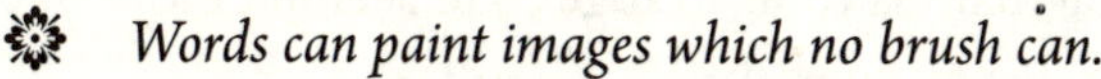

When her love for Krishna had grown tremendously, simply through the medium of words, she realised the power of properly chosen words and the impact they can create in the heart of the listener. Alongside the awakening of her love for Krishna came an unwelcome surprise. Coerced by her brother Rukmi, her father, King Bhishmaka, had chosen the king of Chedi, Shishupala, as her life partner. A person whom she hated from the core of her heart. If Krishna was the abode of good qualities, Shishupala was a garbage dump of bad qualities. Though Rukmi knew that his sister had no interest in marrying Shishupala, he still forced the alliance in order to prove his authority over her and also to use it as a means of securing a political ally. In the grip of blind greed and political ambition, he was ready to ignore the desires of his sister and the will of his father, who was the king of the land.

❁ *You struggle when you suffocate the people you love.*

Rukmini understood that whenever one made the right choices in life, there would always arise challenges that tested one's determination. When one made the wrong choice no challenges arose because making the wrong choice was a compromise in itself. When one made compromises, the pain of that compromise was worse than the anxiety of dealing with the challenge. She knew that time was limited and that she had to act quickly if she wanted to save herself from living a life of compromise. Her own family hadn't allowed her to exercise her choice. Now she decided to express herself completely to someone who was a total stranger. While her family had gifted her hopelessness, that stranger seemed to promise her hope. So though He was actually a total stranger, He seemed more like family than her most intimate family members.

❁ *When you make a choice you also pick a challenge.*
Every compromise to your self-respect is a little move away from yourself.

Considering the distance and the urgency of the situation, Rukmini decided to express herself in the most personal way, using the most impersonal of means. Ideally, she would have loved to do this in person. She wanted to express what was in her heart while looking into His eyes. But that was an impossibility and would have to wait. For now she decided to pour out her heart through the medium of clearly expressed words in a handwritten letter. With tears in her eyes, Rukmini did something that probably no other girl of her era had dared to do. This was probably the riskiest thing she would ever do in her life. But as she carefully etched her heart's message onto that silken cloth, she didn't really feel it was a risk but rather that it was the most natural thing to do. The thoughts flowed as freely from her mind as words flowed freely into the letter, as tears flowed freely from her eyes. As she was writing, she was meditating on the beauty of Krishna. What she felt for Him was something she had never ever felt for anyone.

'O most handsome one, from the moment the ambrosia of your glorious qualities flowed into my ears, my mind has become utterly absorbed in you, O Krishna.' Rukmini blushed as soon as she had written these words. As she stared at the golden letters strewn on the black velvet cloth, she began to think about how Krishna would react upon reading these words. Wouldn't He think how He could possibly accept a king's daughter whom He had never seen or heard of and who was bold enough to write a letter proposing to Him? 'You may think that I am shameless for expressing myself so clearly to a stranger. But let me tell You that I have given myself completely to You in my heart and whether You accept me or reject me is completely Your choice. If You accept me, then I will live a life of joy and gratitude. If You reject me, then I will immediately die with the hope of obtaining You in a future life. In my present condition, there is no question of fear or embarrassment anymore. Simply by hearing about Your good qualities, my mind has become completely attached to You. It's not entirely my fault that I have become so brazen. It's Your fault too. If You didn't have such amazing qualities, then I would not have been so madly attracted to You. So please don't criticise me for my openness.'

 *Self-expression is the voice of the heart that sometimes speaks the language of art, sometimes the language of words, sometimes the language of action and sometimes the language of silence.*

'If You want to know why I chose You as opposed to numerous other men who may also have attractive forms and qualities, then let me explain what makes You unique to me. Your form is the sweetest and most attractive, like a subtle fragrance. An assortment of colours decorates Your beautiful body. There are blues like sapphires, there are pinks like lotuses, there are golden yellows, ruby reds, moonstone whites and midnight blacks. Which other man exists in all of creation with such exquisitely beautiful limbs, lips, hair, nails and form? As much as Your form is beautiful, that much if not more is Your character, graceful. You are the repository of supreme knowledge, wealth, influence and youthfulness. Your very presence creates delight in all mankind. Any unmarried girl who hears about You would definitely want to surrender her life to You and choose You as her life partner. If You are thinking why no other girl has so far been as forward in expressing herself as me, let me tell You that right now it's my marriageable age; when it's their turn they will surely follow suit. I have already chosen You as my husband and I have surrendered myself to You. I request You to come and swiftly whisk me away from this hollow world I live in and take me to the world brimming with love that You live in. I have expressed myself completely to You, my dear Krishna. I offer my body, mind and soul to You forever. If You do not accept me then You must know that I wouldn't want to belong to anyone else, even if it was Lord Brahma. Then what can I say of a jackal like Shishupala?

'If You are inclined to accept me, please come immediately before it's too late. If You desire to whisk me away, then here is a plan that would cause the least damage to my relatives and yet achieve our goal. You should come to the city of Vidarbha on the pretext of attending my wedding ceremony. When You come with a peaceful demeanour, You will be welcomed without anyone suspecting you. Just before the ceremony, I will have to visit the temple of Goddess Girija, which is located on the outskirts of the city. That would be the best place to take me away.'

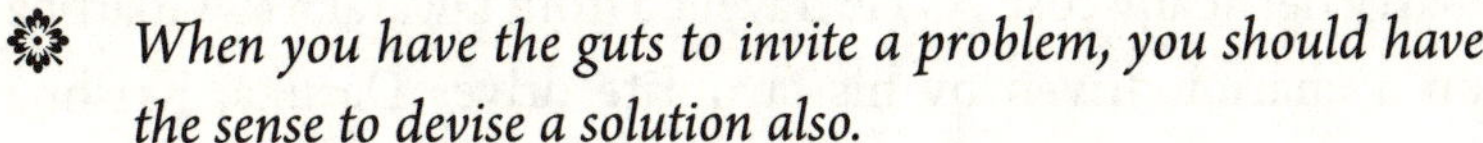

When you have the guts to invite a problem, you should have the sense to devise a solution also.

Tears flowed freely from Krishna's eyes. The brahmana whom Rukmini had so trustingly engaged to bring that most confidential letter to Krishna had just finished reading it out to Him. The brahmana was so grateful to just be a part of this divine connect. He was in fact most surprised when Krishna told him to read out the contents of the letter that Rukmini had sent with Him. He was touched by the fact that both Rukmini and Krishna had shown such immense trust in him. The humble brahmana knew he had been chosen to be the connect between the two. He hadn't chosen this service himself but the service had chosen him. Perhaps his only qualification was his simplicity of heart.

❁ *Connectors are like simple children who intuitively know how to connect two pieces of a puzzle. Just by making those small connections between like-minded people, they unknowingly become architects of a powerful, well-networked society.*

'Rukmini is as pure as firewood. Just by hearing her words, I can clearly make out the purity of her heart and intentions. I will kindle the fire within that firewood to burn up the impurities in the form of the bad kings that have assembled there. She has dedicated herself exclusively to Me; I will surely set out for Vidarbha right away and bring her to Dwaraka after slaying those dastardly kings in battle. Just as she has heard about Me, I have heard about her. Rukmini possesses intelligence, beauty, auspiciousness, good character and every other good quality one could hope for in a life partner.' Krishna became determined to marry her at any cost. As He travelled from Dwaraka to Vidarbha on a chariot driven by his favourite driver Daruka, Krishna was lost in thought. Rukmini's beautifully expressed words kept ringing in His mind. He held the letter tightly in His fist, clutching it as if His life depended on it. Tears flowed freely as the chariot sped towards Vidarbha.

The preparations for the wedding were on at full speed. Just a few more minutes and everything would be over for Rukmini. She had a back-up plan for how she would end her life in case Krishna didn't make it, but that was for later. Right now there was hope. As she was being readied in her wedding finery, Rukmini had a serene look on her face. No distorted lines of agony appeared on her beautiful face yet. Though she was extremely worried, she was still hopeful. Just then, from the corner of her eye, she spotted a silhouette in the corner of the room, reflected in her mirror. She swung around in anticipation. Looking back at her was the brahmana she had sent with her letter. He was all smiles. She blushed and a subtle smile appeared on her face for a moment. A confirmation! Steadying herself, she hid her smile. With a slight nod of her head she acknowledged the contribution of this man in her life. For now this was all she could offer him. The situation was too delicate to do anything that would arouse suspicion. She didn't want to make it difficult for Krishna. If she survived this, she could reward the brahmana at an appropriate time.

> *What is the use of a lamp without darkness? What is the use of hope without tremendous anxiety? Only in the midst of the greatest negativity is there scope to exhibit the greatest positivity.*

Standing up abruptly, she began to walk out of the palace. She mounted a palanquin, which conveyed her to the historical temple of Devi Girija. There was a bounce in her steps, worry in her mind, hope in her heart and a prayer on her lips. It was the only prayer that she would ever have in her life—let her be united with Krishna forever. No other prayer seemed meaningful. No other desire seemed worthy. As she exited the prayer hall of the temple, she saw an entire army standing in front of her. It stretched in a semi-circle all across the vacant garden in front of her as far as her eye could see. Mounted on chariots, elephants and horses were numerous kings who had come to attend the royal wedding. Rather than a plethora of kings, it simply seemed like a gathering of goons to her. There were Jarasandha, Shishupala, Rukmi, and all their friends, who in Rukmini's opinion were nothing more than royal bullies with no heart.

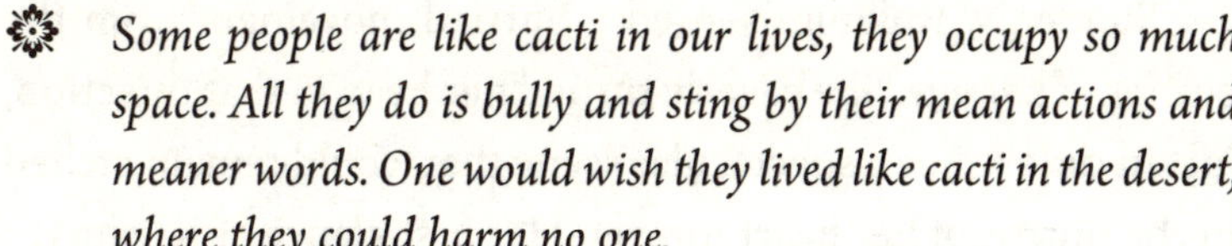

> *Some people are like cacti in our lives, they occupy so much space. All they do is bully and sting by their mean actions and meaner words. One would wish they lived like cacti in the desert, where they could harm no one.*

Her eyes kept scanning the crowd for someone. Someone she had never seen before. A stranger who would be more familiar than all those she knew in front of her. As her eyes scanned the crowds, a cry went up from the assembled gathering. The kings who had assembled had been waiting for their first glimpse of the divine beauty of Rukmini. They had all heard numerous tales of her beauty. This was the first time they were going to glimpse it first-hand. As soon as their gaze fell on Rukmini's exquisite beauty, their minds went numb. Some eyes remained fixed on Rukmini's winged earrings, which were constantly kissing her cheeks. They couldn't look away. Some eyes were riveted on her bejewelled waistband. Some eyes were fixed on the endearing lock of hair that kept swinging in front of her eyes. Some eyes were totally engrossed in the row of pearl-like teeth that peeked out only occasionally. Some eyes were transfixed by the tinkling anklet that adorned her feet. No eye was able to absorb everything about her persona. Whatever little it was able to observe was more than enough to drown it in a pool of ecstasy. An involuntary gasp emanated from the mouths of the kings. Lust tore at their hearts like an animal ripping the flesh off its prey. Every one of them dropped their weapons. While these kings were being mesmerised by Rukmini's beauty, Rukmini was brushing the hair from her eyes. The moment she did that, many began to swoon and fall out of their vehicles. Some even fell off their elephants.

Suddenly, Rukmini sensed a hurried movement from the corner of her eye. She eagerly turned her head in that direction, just in time to see a spectacular scene that would remain etched in the mirror of her heart forever. Her first glance at Krishna!

Krishna shot out of the crowd, riding a golden chariot

bearing the emblem of Garuda on a flag, drawn by five splendid horses, with a peacock feather adorning His crown, a silken yellow dhoti around His waist, and shining golden armour covering His broad chest. With the reigns gripped in His strong hands, the speed at which His chariot moved was unbelievable. It almost seemed to float above the ground. In a flash He was right in front of her. Looking straight into her eyes, He placed His hand around her waist and gently lifted her onto the chariot. He continued to gaze at her as He drove off. Rukmini lost herself in the ocean of Krishna's eyes.

She was rudely shaken from her reverie by an arrow that zoomed through the narrow gap between their faces, embedding itself on the chariot mast. That's when reality dawned on her. This wasn't going to be easy at all. Fear took over instantly. Soon hundreds of arrows whizzed past the eloping couple, coming from all directions. As Krishna focussed on putting as much distance as possible between themselves and their attackers, Rukmini focussed on Krishna's serene face. Even in the midst of such danger, there was not a trace of worry on His face. But rather a subtle smile that was characteristic of Him.

❁ *Just as the smile of the crescent moon against the backdrop of utter darkness is most beautiful, the smile on the face of a person who is surrounded by unlimited troubles is the most attractive.*

Suddenly an unknown army intervened between Krishna's chariot and the army of enemies who was chasing them. Everyone came to a screeching halt. Rukmini was totally confused, seeing this third army. Who were they? What were they doing here in the midst of a private affair? As numerous questions popped up in her mind, she looked at Krishna in concern. Krishna smiled brilliantly, sensing her worry. Then He said something that was unbelievable to her. Those words meant everything to Rukmini. Those words assured Rukmini that she had indeed chosen the most perfect partner for life. Someone who could express such feelings in words could capture the heart. She had always believed that words were the key to the human heart. That's precisely why she chose to write that letter in the first place.

❁ *Words play with the ball of emotions in the playground of our hearts in the game of love.*
Choose words well to win the game of love.

With a smile on his face, holding Rukmini close to His heart, and gazing into her eyes, Krishna said, 'O most beautiful, delicate princess Rukmini, give up your fear now. "Your" army will take care of our enemies.'

In an instant all her fears vanished and a radiant smile decorated her beautiful face. Krishna knew exactly how to win hearts. In that one sentence Rukmini was bowled over. What a subtle message it was! By saying 'your army' Krishna had made Rukmini a part of His family and the owner of everything He possessed, even before officially marrying her. That one gesture touched her so deeply. She had already decided to dedicate this life to Him, but now she decided to dedicate every single one of her lives to Him.

Krishna's Yadava army did its job, while Krishna whisked Rukmini off to Dwaraka.

❁ *False love is like a fountain, it seems to be giving out everything but in reality taking it all back.*

True love is like a waterfall, it gives everything while expecting nothing.

❧

What a story! What a connection! What an understanding of loving communication! Arjuna was enthralled by his friend's fantastic adventure. An adventure that had led to this beautiful understanding of how to connect with the person you love on the deepest level, through artful expressions of love. Just as Arjuna was appreciating the wisdom in Krishna's story, he was stumped by a suggestion from Krishna.

He couldn't believe that Krishna had actually suggested that! He was confused yet pleased at the same time. Krishna had suggested that Arjuna could find happiness similar to His own if he eloped with Krishna's sister Subhadra. He had no idea how Krishna knew of his secret desire to make Subhadra his wife. However, Balaram, Krishna's older brother, had decided to bestow her hand on his disciple Duryodhana, without knowing that she had no interest in the alliance.

Krishna shared his master plan with Arjuna, while descending the high Raivataka mountains where they had been having this secret meeting of theirs for the last few hours. It was simple, yet hilarious and very dangerous. Arjuna had no idea how he was going to pull off the dangerously naughty prank that Krishna proposed to him. The first half of the plan was to find out if Subhadra was actually as interested in Arjuna as he was in her. If she was, then the rest of the plan would be much simpler to execute.

 *Whether it is in a circus or in life, jokes have their price. The only difference is that in a circus the joker gets paid and in life the joker pays a price.*

Arjuna proceeded to Prabhasa and Krishna proceeded towards Dwaraka. In a few days, Krishna planned a visit to the Prabhasa area along with all his family members. He made sure that Balaram joined them as well. Once they were there, amongst the plethora of sages that had assembled to carry out their chaturmasa observation (severe austerities during the four months of the rainy season), Krishna took His family towards a particular pre-decided location. There, on a rocky surface, sat a stern-looking sage. Dressed in radiant saffron attire, wearing holy markings on twelve parts of his body, the holy tridanda staff (a combination of three sticks held by a renunciant, indicating dedication of body, mind and words) leaning on one shoulder, the sacred thread running across his torso, seated in lotus position with an erect back, eyes closed and hands joined in supplication, this handsome sage was intensity personified.

Balaram was highly impressed; He was all praise, appreciating the attitude of renunciation displayed by the sage at such a young age. Krishna burst out laughing. When He realised that Balaram was glaring at Him in anger, He controlled His laughter. Balaram was annoyed at Krishna's untimely jokes. Krishna assumed a very serious demeanour but couldn't suppress occasional smiles. Arjuna was a million times better than He had imagined!

 *Suppressing anything only magnifies its intensity. When you suppress pain, it leaks out as a tear. When you suppress a smile, it flowers forth as laughter.*

Balaram offered His respects by bowing to the holy one. The sage, in turn, immediately offered his respects to Balaram. When Balaram questioned him, he said that one should always bow to a person who possesses great qualities. That one statement pleased Balaram so much He decided to invite this sage to Dwaraka to spend the next four months in Their care. He also announced that His sister Subhadra would personally take care of the sage while he performed his severe austerities.

❁ *Praise is the master key to all locks of the heart.*

As soon as He heard that, Krishna pulled His brother aside. Krishna spoke animatedly, with a look of concern, 'How can you do this? Look at this sage. He is so young, handsome, strong-looking and possesses extremely attractive features. More than anything else, look at his ability to talk sweetly. How can you allow our unmarried sister to associate with him for four months? It could be a disaster.'

'Stop doubting everything, Krishna! You always think the opposite of what I think. Why should We doubt an exalted self-controlled sage like this? Can't you discern from his mannerisms that he is genuine? Where do we find such respectful and respectable people today? Don't you know how auspicious it is for a maiden girl to serve a sage during his chaturmasa vrata? Narada became the son of Brahma simply by serving the sages during the chaturmasa period in his previous life. Even our aunt Kunti achieved the greatest benediction from Durvasa muni after sincerely serving him during his chaturmasa period. Don't worry, I know what I am doing. Nothing will go wrong as long as I am around,' Balaram concluded and walked away, leaving Krishna smiling His naughty smile. Sometimes reverse psychology is the best way to get people to do what you want them to do!

 *The more you take something away from a child, the more he clutches at it. Using reverse psychology works just as well with adults as children. The more you try to persuade a person to not do something, the child-like nature in him tries to hook on to that very thing.*

Returning to the sage, Balaram instructed His men to arrange to take the sage to Dwaraka. He went on to appreciate Subhadra's good fortune in getting this rare heaven-sent opportunity to exclusively focus on taking care of this holy person in the next four months. He instructed Krishna to supervise all arrangements, including putting up the sage near Subhadra's palace and ensuring that everything was in order. Krishna bent slightly, acknowledging and accepting His role, saying, 'O elder brother, Your wish is My command!'

As soon as the sage, who in reality was Arjuna in disguise, entered the serene abode that had been created for him in Dwaraka, his eyes fell on Subhadra. Her exquisite beauty completely bewitched him. Noticing Arjuna staring at Subhadra openly, Krishna nudged him before his sister could notice his odd behaviour. Getting back his composure, Arjuna began to focus on his act yet again. Handing over all responsibilities to Subhadra, Krishna instructed her that she should take utmost care of the sanyasi and ensure that his every need was taken care of. He warned her not to be negligent in her services. Krishna also informed her that the sage was highly knowledgeable and was a repository of the most amazing stories from the scriptures. He told her to take full advantage of his presence and make sure that she heard as much as possible, every single day of his stay in Dwaraka.

Subhadra immediately launched herself into taking care of the august sage. She was highly meticulous with all the arrangements. Even before the sage expressed a need, she had already anticipated it and made the necessary arrangements. Arjuna was highly impressed with her proactive intelligence. He spent hours every day narrating fantastic stories to her that made her laugh and cry. He was definitely an orator par excellence. She began to love these story-telling sessions and would eagerly wait for that time of the day. Four months passed in quick succession. As the rains poured outside, the peacock of Arjuna's heart was dancing inside. Every single moment spent in Subhadra's company convinced him that she was the person he wanted to love for the rest of his life. Though he maintained a respectful distance, not wanting to tarnish the role he was playing, nonetheless, in his heart he relished her company.

❁ *Story telling is like colouring wax. First it melts you, then it adds colour to your life and then it shapes the new you.*

At the end of the rainy season, Balaram went on a pilgrimage with the whole family and all the Yadava leaders. Since the guest sage had to remain in Dwaraka to complete the final rituals of the chaturmasa period, Subhadra had to stay back to take care of him. Arjuna had to ascertain if she was interested in the alliance in this window of time. The clarification he wanted arrived unsought.

Once her relatives departed from Dwaraka, Subhadra requested an audience with the sage and asked him an interesting question. She wanted to know if during his travels to so many places, he had ever come across the Pandavas. When he replied in the affirmative she continued her questions. Initially, she asked indirect questions, trying to get him to say something specific that she wanted to hear. But when she realised he wasn't taking the bait, she decided to ask directly.

'In all your travels to so many holy places did you meet Arjuna, who I heard is also visiting all the holy places in his time of exile?' Subhadra's face reddened the moment she took Arjuna's name. Looking down, she began to scratch the floor with her toe nails, restlessly awaiting his answer. This came as a pleasant surprise to Arjuna. This was more than a clear indication.

He said, 'Yes, I met him.'

Subhadra jumped up the next moment, asking where he had met Arjuna. He replied with one word. 'Here,' he said, with a mischievous smile.

Initially, she wasn't able to comprehend what he meant. But when the truth dawned on her, her mouth popped open wide in surprise. Her eyes took in his beautiful form with great attention. Arjuna stood with his hands on his hips, smiling naughtily. Covering her gaping mouth with her hands, Subhadra blushed. She hadn't expected it to happen in this way. Though she had given her heart to Arjuna just by hearing about his good qualities, she hadn't ever seen him in person. In the last four months that she had been serving him so closely in the form of a sanyasi, she hadn't ever looked at him openly. As soon as she realised that this was the same person she had longed to associate with, she felt ecstatic.

Folding his hands across his chest, Arjuna smiled at her, raising his eyebrows questioningly. She looked at him shyly and raised her eyebrows, asking him what he wanted. He asked her, 'Now how do we take things ahead?'

She said, 'I don't take such decisions. Ask my brother Krishna.'

Arjuna's smile broadened on hearing Krishna's name. If only she knew that the master planner of this whole scheme was the very person whose approval she sought.

'Assuming that Krishna approves, then will you come with me?' Arjuna teased her further.

'Even if Krishna approves, my parents should agree.' Subhadra teased him back. She wasn't going to give in so easily.

'What if your parents also agree, will you marry me?' Arjuna pushed for a definite answer.

❁ *When you help others make their decisions in life, the first thing you have to ensure is that you don't project your decision as their decision.*

Decision-making is essentially a combination of four things: weighing options, clarifying assumptions, considering long-term repercussions and preparing to be wrong.

Now Subhadra had no answer, except to smile bashfully. Just then Krishna entered the chamber, accompanied by Vasudev and Devaki. Running into Devaki's arms, Subhadra hid her face. The three of them blessed her profusely and encouraged her to listen to her heart. Subhadra looked shyly at Arjuna. Their eyes met. The full moon of Subhadra's eyes created a tidal wave of emotions in the oceanic heart of Arjuna and vice versa. When their emotions settled, Arjuna held out his hand and Subhadra happily accepted it.

Krishna informed Arjuna that His chariot was stationed outside the palace and was at his disposal. After saying that, Krishna departed along with Vasudev and Devaki, giving the couple some privacy. Subhadra was thrilled to be in the company of the person she admired so much for all the wonderful qualities she had heard tales about. Added to her previous quota of stories about Arjuna were another four months of private stories that none other than she knew. She felt blessed to have spent four months with him, albeit unknowingly. In these four months, she realised that Arjuna had done something magical. Through the medium of words he had conveyed so much to her. Using stories as a tool, he had shared the blueprint of how an ideal human should be and how ideal relationships work and how they fail. She had received the opportunity to hear from Arjuna and understand his mindset completely. Now she felt that she was very much in sync with him and well equipped to enter the ocean of his love.

❁ *The most important thing that helps one sail through tough times in relationships is sifting through the treasured database of private memories.*

Subhadra was so thrilled to know that her life was practically running parallel to her brother's. Even her love story was running on the same track as her brother's. But more than anything else, she was happy to hear that Krishna had actually prepared Arjuna well before he actually entered into this relationship with His sister. For a woman, the heartfelt expression of words in a relationship is more important than anything else. She was delighted to find that her brother had trained her to-be husband well.

❁ *To enter into some relationships you have to prepare yourself the way you prepare to enter a hazardous chemical lab. Be careful of being infected.*

To enter into some relationships you have to prepare yourself the way you prepare to enter an intensive care unit at a hospital. Be careful of an infection.

To enter into some relationships you have to neither prepare nor be prepared. Entering these relationships is like going home, where you don't need to prepare to give or receive love.

There was a commotion in Subhadra's palace. What on earth was going on? The guards were dumbfounded! The sage who had been peacefully performing his religious rites for the last four months was now mounted on a chariot, wearing golden armour on his chest and holding a bow in his hand. What was most astounding was that in his other hand was the hand of the princess, who was driving the chariot. The whole scene was so confusing that the guards had no idea what to make of it or even what they were supposed to do. Suddenly, a guard cried out, 'Stop him! The cheater is kidnapping our princess!'

❁ *Many a time, deception is simply incorrect perception.*

Though it didn't really seem like a kidnapping but rather an elopement, the guard's cry had caught on and everyone began to rally to stop the kidnapping. Soon hundreds of arrows were zooming past the fleeing couple. Arjuna and Subhadra smiled at each other. Now their story was completely in sync with Krishna's story. Arjuna began to effortlessly shoot arrows and thwart all the efforts of the numerous soldiers who were attacking from all directions. Not even for a moment did his eyes leave Subhadra's. His hands were fighting and her hands were driving, but their eyes were busy in a soul-searching exercise.

She was so grateful to her brother, who had played such an integral part in bringing about this union. She realised that He had planned everything to perfection. As she was driving the chariot, she recollected that Krishna had insisted on teaching her how to drive a chariot. He had made sure that she knew both the gross form of chariot driving and also the subtle aspects that very few knew. A tear escaped her eye as she gazed at Arjuna in the midst of the plethora of arrows whizzing by. Nothing else mattered to her and no one else mattered to her, except these two people, the one whom she had given her life to and the one who gave her a new life.

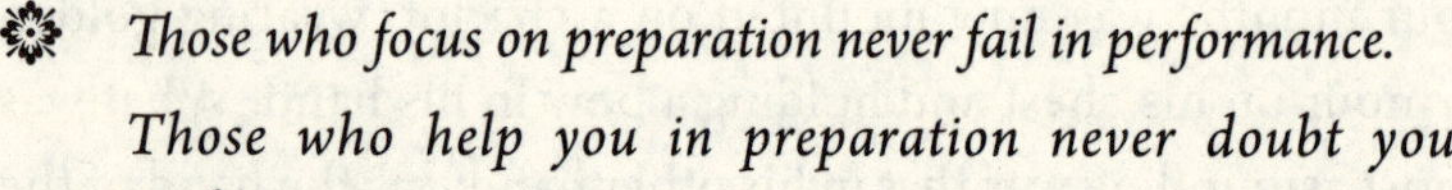

Those who focus on preparation never fail in performance.

Those who help you in preparation never doubt your performance.

While Arjuna was countering the arrows of the Yadava soldiers and destroying their defences, the soldiers observed a very interesting phenomenon. Arjuna's arrows were being shot in such a way that they were destroying their weapons and chariots but not harming any of the soldiers. In fact, none even had a single bruise on their body, even though the arrows passed them so closely. Arjuna was such an archery expert that he ensured no one was harmed in the slightest. The soldiers continued to chase the chariot, which was moving at the speed of the mind. When they reached the borders of Dwaraka, they lost track of the chariot as it seemed to have vanished mysteriously. In fact, they couldn't even trace the marks of the tyres. They were clueless about how that could have happened. On returning to the palace they raised an alarm and reported the whole incident to Balaram, who had just returned from the pilgrimage.

Balaram was totally bewildered on hearing the news of His sister's kidnapping. Though He was boiling in anger, He instructed the soldiers to find out Krishna's opinion in this matter. When everyone turned to Krishna, they found Him seated with His head held in His hands in great anxiety and pain. His whole body was shaking violently. They felt that He was crying out of desperation. In reality, Krishna was trying to control His laughter. Try as He might, He was unable to resist laughing out loud. So the only way out was to hide His face in His palms and laugh His heart out. Once He got his mirth under control He said, 'I had warned My elder brother right at the beginning not to trust this person. But He didn't heed My advice. I carried out His instructions, since He is My older brother. And now look at the price We have had to pay for that oversight. Let Me explain My understanding of the situation at hand. Listen carefully.' All the Yadava leaders including Balaram listened intently to Krishna.

❁ *When the master of words plays with people's hearts and minds, it is called a masterstroke.*

'According to My sources, this imposter of a sage was none other than Arjuna, the Pandava prince.' As soon as Krishna said that, everyone gasped. Balaram was furious at Arjuna's audacity. How could he have duped them like that? He was angrier at Himself for not having recognised him in spite of him staying with them for four whole months. But He bit his lips and controlled His anger, allowing Krishna to continue speaking.

'At this point we have two choices. One is to go ahead and fight with Arjuna and bring back our sister. But this choice is very risky considering the fact that Arjuna is invincible even when alone. We then have to consider our chances if he manages to reach Indraprastha and invites Bhima to join him in the fight. If we are defeated, it will bring great infamy to Dwaraka. Moreover, after coming into contact with Arjuna and being with him for such a long time, who will marry our sister, even if we manage to bring her back? The second option therefore is to invite Arjuna to marry Subhadra ourselves. After all, there can be no better match for our sister than the mighty Arjuna. His knowledge is infinite, being the grandson of Vyasdev. His strength is infinite, being the son of Indra. Moreover his character is impeccable, being the son of our maternal aunt Kunti. Ideally, knowing all this about Arjuna, we should have taken the proposal to him in the first place. But now that he himself has kidnapped Subhadra, we have lost that chance. If we fight him and lose, we will lose whatever little is left of our reputation. So if you carefully analyse the chances of victory or defeat, either way is going to be a defeat for us if we pick a fight with Arjuna. My suggestion is that we invite Arjuna to marry Subhadra.'

❁ *When you don't make choices, life will not give you options.*

As the Yadava leaders were trying to weigh the two options Krishna had placed in front of them, Krishna played His masterstroke. 'Oh by the way, did any of you notice that Arjuna was not driving the chariot?' This caught everyone off-guard. They looked at Krishna in puzzlement. 'Actually, Subhadra was driving the chariot. Which means that this was not a case of kidnapping, but rather a case of elopement.'

Balaram sat back down on His throne. That was the last thing He had expected to hear. There was nothing left to discuss now. His sister had run away with Arjuna willingly. What was the point in discussing options?

❁ *To accept reality one needs dignity and humility. Dignity to stand after a fall and humility to say, 'I tried.'*

Taking a plethora of priceless gifts with them, Balaram and Krishna set out from Dwaraka. Tracking down Arjuna and Subhadra, They requested Arjuna to accept Their sister as his wife. Arjuna in turn begged forgiveness for having misled Them in such a manner in these last four months. Falling at Their feet, he explained to Them that his only intention had been to win Subhadra's hand. Before marrying her, he needed to affirm if she was the right match for him and more than that if she was really interested in him. Balaram embraced Arjuna and forgave him promptly. The wedding took place with great pomp and festivity.

Arjuna and Subhadra walked up to Krishna and Rukmini after the wedding ceremony. All four broke out into big smiles. This was a secret they would hold in their hearts forever. But more secretive than this secret plan was the secret that they had learnt about how relationships thrive. The secret of the power of expressing oneself! Subhadra was grateful to Arjuna for teaching her this secret. Arjuna was grateful to Krishna for teaching him this secret. Krishna was grateful to Rukmini for teaching Him this secret. And Rukmini was grateful to her heart for allowing her to learn this secret.

APPRECIATIVE EXPRESSIONS OF LOVE

The tongue is probably God's most delicate creation. If it unfurls to hurl distasteful words, it can break the bonds of the strongest relationship. If it twirls to spread gentle words, it can enhance the weakest. Verbal expressions are game changers. Thus the tongue and the words that spill out of the tongue have to be monitored with discernment.

This story explores the power of words in relationships. The world knows Krishna to be a master of words but this story describes Rukmini's mastery over the world of words. Love is a very important element in life. But expressing that love is more crucial. The story begins with Rukmini taking the step of expressing her love through a letter. Whether it is verbally or through the written word, expressions of love have to be conveyed in the right tone.

People invest more energy in not expressing their love than in expressing it. They avoid expressing their feelings due to hidden fears, encouraged by popular beliefs about relationships, which tell people that the goal of relationships is to obtain happiness and happiness lies in receiving, not in giving. When this thought is ingrained in a person, they look for attention, love, respect and appreciation from the people they love rather than focusing on giving the same. The fear is if they give first, then they won't get enough in return, that those who give end up as losers.

In this story, Rukmini expresses very honestly to Krishna what His love meant for her and the effect that simply hearing about Him had on her. Her world was a painful one, where everyone including her father and brother placed their needs above hers. She said that the outer layer of her consciousness had been severely dented, which was manifesting itself as dents in her inner layer. What she needed was warmth to light her up inside. In the midst of such pain, the only thing that was inspiring her to continue living was the hope of receiving Krishna's love.

When people feel loveable, that knowledge helps them deal with everything painful in life. Loving someone is a privilege and telling them about your love is a gift. Not expressing your love is taking the relationship for granted. No one has ever had a problem with an over-expression of love, but under-expression definitely feels like daily death. For love to grow, one should be stingy with criticism and generous with appreciation. Unfortunately, many of us don't understand enough the power of generosity with words.

People tend to act in accordance with the way they are treated. If you treat them with generous words of appreciation, rest assured you are in for a treat. Criticism attracts criticism. Generosity attracts generosity. When you are generous with your words of appreciation, you are subtly telling yourself that you are rich and therefore can afford to be generous with your words. When you are stingy with your words of appreciation, you are subtly telling yourself that when you yourself are a beggar, how can you afford to be generous towards others? The language you speak is the language in which you think. Generosity with words requires no resources but only a loving heart.

Your vocabulary is not formed with words but with intentions. When words are woven in an intricate, loving way, they permanently embroider the design of love in the fabric of your heart. Thus Rukmini's words affected Krishna. He decided to drop everything He was doing to reciprocate her love. Following the plan that Rukmini had suggested to Him, Krishna came at the right moment and whisked her away. When all the kings attacked the eloping couple, there was fear in Rukmini's eyes. The first words that came from Krishna's mouth convinced her that she had made the right choice in taking such a risk. With just a few words, Krishna not only allayed her doubts and gave her hope but also touched the deepest chords in her heart. Krishna was so generous with his words that Rukmini's heart began dancing.

Small gestures impact relationships much more than big gifts. When people focus on the big gifts and in the process neglect the small gestures, they may find their relationships failing. Human beings are social animals. They thrive on love. Though one may focus on giving expensive gifts to the one they love, they forget to find out what that person is actually seeking. One can live without gifts but one cannot live without love. One tends to forget that people whom we love need our expressions of love to feel an emotional connect even if there is physical contact. People need daily quota of loving words to gently remind them that they are loveable. This ensures their emotional health and stability. The feeling of being loveable is something that no gift can replace.

Through Krishna, Arjuna learnt the art of loving expressions. Rukmini triggered Krishna's love through written words. Arjuna triggered Subhadra's love through spoken words. Love is not just words but actions that back up those words. Rukmini, Krishna, Arjuna and Subhadra not only expressed loving words but took actions that backed up each word they spoke. Words lose their meaning if they are not aligned with actions. Authenticity in relationships comes when two people express their emotions lovingly and act sincerely to serve and encourage each other to reach their potential.

Rukmini never demanded but requested Krishna's love. Arjuna never demanded but requested Subhadra's love. Krishna never expected anything from Rukmini but empathised with her and encouraged her. Subhadra never expected anything from Arjuna but was kind to him and served him. Loving words need not only be romantic in nature. They could encompass requests, empathy, encouragement and kindness. When the right words are showered on people, there will be a tsunami of love coming your way. Why should we settle for bits of love when there is a full tidal wave waiting to be explored?

Chapter 3

A SILENT VOICE

'Stop! Don't shoot!' A sharp voice wound through the woods and embedded itself in King Dushyanta's ears. The voice was so authoritative that the chivalrous king immediately put his bow down and touched his driver's shoulder. The next instant the chariot came to a screeching halt. Anticipating the sudden jerk, the king had caught hold of the mast of the chariot to stop himself from toppling over. Jumping off, he walked in the direction of the voice. From the corner of his eyes, the king could discern the silhouette of a deer, which was sprinting away, grateful to still be alive.

❁ *Death is God's way of teaching gratitude for life.*

From the moment King Dushyanta had entered the forest, he had been on a high-octane hunting spree. He had first set his eyes on this beautiful doe just a few minutes ago. The moment he spotted her a few miles away from where he now stood, he felt that there was a karmic bond between him and the innocent doe. He instantly felt pulled towards her. Directing his driver to take him closer, the king readied himself for hot pursuit. The doe was relishing some tender grass when she heard the rumble of chariot wheels. The moment she turned around, the half-chewed clump of green grass dropped from her mouth, which fell open at the scene that greeted her. For a moment she froze. The next moment she fled. While running she would turn around obliquely and cast a glance at her pursuers every few seconds. King Dushyanta stood at the back of the chariot, drunk on speed and savouring the adrenaline rush in his veins. She could hear the harsh voice of the chariot driver urging his horses on.

❁ *Destiny is the meeting point of disappointment and hope.*

Dushyanta loved the extreme sensations that an unbridled chase caused in him. This was a totally different world. Everything around him including the trees, rocks, his own chariot and even his bow seemed transformed into elongated objects made even more impressive by the thunderous gallop of his horses. All notion of distance disappeared. Speed swallowed everything. The only thing that existed was a question of far or near. As the chariot neared the trembling, sweat-drenched doe, the king notched an arrow onto his bow and readied himself to let it fly. That's when he heard that commanding voice ordering him to stop. The power in that voice had forced him to drop his bow instantly and abandon his mission.

❁ *When discrimination is lost in the inner noise, you need an outer voice to wake you upto the realities of life.*

As the horses stood shaking their manes, expressing their displeasure at this unexpected halt, the king walked towards the source of the sound. From within the woods emerged two venerable sages. They appeared scholarly and their frail frames signified their austere lifestyle. The one who appeared a bit more senior spoke as he walked, 'Do not harm such a sweet-natured animal. Only the cruel destroy delicate flowers by setting them alight. Power should be used to protect the weak, not harm them. O King, you have been chosen by the gods to protect the meek and innocent. Use your powers with discrimination.'

So what if he was the king of the land? The truth, when spoken, applied to all. This was such a refreshing experience for Dushyanta. The king was used to people eulogising him and praising every single thing he did. But here was a simple man with the audacity to instruct him so frankly, yet the king didn't feel any anger. In fact, he felt grateful for having had the good fortune to meet such straightforward people, who did not mince their words just because he was the king. Joining his hands, he dropped his bow and prostrated himself before them. Pleased with the compliant attitude of such a powerful king, the sages blessed him saying that he would have a son who would rule the world. It seemed as if the sounds of the forest had all been funnelled into the words that had just been uttered. There was complete silence as Dushyanta savoured the moment.

❁ *Fortunate are those who have someone to help them discriminate right from wrong. Even more fortunate are those who have the discrimination to discriminate whether to follow that advice or not.*

When Dushyanta stood up, he noticed that a few other sages had also joined them. Together they informed him that he had inadvertently entered the gates of the hermitage of the great Sage Kanva who had gone on a pilgrimage. The sage had departed after handing over the responsibility of taking care of any guests to his daughter Shakuntala. They urged Dushyanta to step into the ashram and delight in the peace and tranquillity that was to be found in abundance there. They told him that he deserved a few moments of peace and solitude, given his complicated and highly demanding lifestyle.

❁ *Just as the value of a flame is greatest in the darkness, similarly the value of peace is greatest in the midst of complications.*

Unable to deny such an offer, Dushyanta chose to enter the hermitage and spend some time soaking in the sanctity of the space. It was as if the open gates resembled outstretched arms inviting him in. It was almost as if the arms of destiny were welcoming him towards his future. Everything seemed to have been predestined. His coming to the forest on that particular day, choosing that particular deer to chase, being led by the deer in that direction, being stopped at the nick of time by the sages, being invited by the sages to enter the ashram and actually deciding to do it. He decided to enter the holy premises in a humble state of mind. Taking off his armour, armlets, belt, necklace, crown and anklets, he handed them over to his chariot driver. While walking towards the gates of the ashram, accompanied by the sages, the king felt as if he was walking towards the heavens.

❁ *There are landmark events that make us and there are landmark events that break us. Both kinds of events together shape us.*

Allowing the king some privacy in that holy setting on the banks of the Malini River, the sages walked away to resume their duties. The king realised that there were many moments in which he had wished that he could be in a solitary place far away from the pressures of ruling a kingdom and dealing with people. A place where he could simply be a human being and enjoy the freshness of nature. A place where he would not have to deal with the artificial smiles of people who seemed to worship him but secretly harboured negativity in their minds. The gods had granted his unsaid prayer through the medium of an innocent doe, who had led him here.

❁ *A place where you are a nobody is a place where there is no pressure of being a somebody.*

Looking around, Dushyanta concluded that the hermitage was a world of its own. Everything including the sacrificial fires, the fragrant flowering trees, the sages focussed on their meditation, the quietly grazing fawns, the chirping birds and the cool breeze blowing from the river banks exuded purity. The king felt tiny and inconsequential in such a space. He shed his shoes. As soon as his feet touched the moist soil of the hermitage, he felt enlivened. All his exhaustion vanished in an instant. He felt fresh and energetic. Overwhelming emotions gripped him. There was anguish and simultaneously there was delight. He felt that he was walking into the threshold of his destiny.

He looked around at the amazing variety of flowering trees that dotted the ashram gardens. He walked to a jasmine bush and bent to inhale the fragrance of the freshly blooming flowers. Just then he heard a tinkle of sweet laughter to an accompaniment of feminine voices coming his way. He quickly hid himself behind a mango tree. The sight that met his eyes was an enchanting one. It made every definition of beauty he knew of seem pale. The thousands of stunning courtesans in his private chambers seemed insipid in comparison.

He continued to stare at the three young ladies who had

stepped into the garden, dressed in robes of bark and balancing earthen pots on their hips. The curve of the pots seemed to perfectly fit into the curves of their hips. The natural freshness of their looks, the suppleness of their gait and the liveliness of their laughter struck a chord in the depths of the king's heart. This was so different from the calculated mannerisms of the palace and the languid poses of the women there. Of the three, Dushyanta's eyes gravitated towards the one in the middle. Her beauty was unearthly. He wondered if anyone he had ever seen in his life was even remotely as beautiful. The king was mesmerised by this gorgeous damsel. The sweetness of her laughter would put even the sweet singing of birds to shame. He had to pinch himself to check if this was indeed reality or a phantasm encountered in a dream.

❁ *Calculated artificial perfection gets a wow from the lips, while spontaneous natural grace elicits a smile from the soul.*

Unaware of the intruder's presence, the girls were having their fun. 'You two water those plants there and I will manage these here,' the most beautiful one said.

Hearing her instructions one of the other girls remarked jokingly, 'Shakuntala, your father is making such a delicate girl perform such tough tasks. Surely he must have a very hard heart.'

'This is unbelievable! The daughter of Kanva Maharishi is stunning! Even the very name Shakuntala strikes a chord in my heart. Every limb of my body is tingling just by hearing her name and listening to her melodious voice.' Dushyanta was losing his composure in the face of Shakuntala's divine beauty.

'Anusuya, don't disparage my father. He is the most loving person on earth. His compassion is beyond compare. I am only doing this service due to my love for these plants. I consider them to be my siblings. My care for them comes from the heart. When you care for your loved ones, there is no question of it being a burden.' Shakuntala continued to water the plants gracefully as she argued playfully with her friends.

Suddenly Shakuntala turned towards the mango tree behind which Dushyanta was hiding. She led her friends in that direction. Priyamvada asked, 'Anusuya, do you know why Shakuntala is staring at the mango tree?'

Anusuya, who had caught on to her friend's highly charged state of mind said, 'I do not know dear. The mind of our friend is difficult to predict at the moment.'

Priyamvada pointed to the nine-petalled jasmine vine that wound around the mango tree. 'She is running towards the queen of the forest. Do you remember that Shakuntala had anointed the fragrant jasmine vine the queen of the forest? Just like the queen found her king, the mango tree, and is now clinging to him, our dear queen, Shakuntala, is also waiting for her king to come and whisk her away.' Both girls laughed heartily while Shakuntala walked away shyly from their banter.

Dushyanta began to wonder while staring at Shakuntala's beautiful face. His thoughts began to crystallise into a possibility. 'Is it even possible for a sage like Kanva to have a girl as stunningly attractive as this? Neither her looks nor her demeanour seem in any way priestly. She looks exalted enough to be the queen of a royal dynasty. If she was from a priestly background, why is my warrior heart getting helplessly enamoured of her? When there is uncertainty, men of substance allow their inner voice to guide them in making the right choices. But though the clarion call of my inner voice is so clear in this matter, I still need to determine the reality of her origins.'

❁ *Your inner voice is positivity trying to tell you something.*

When you learn to filter out the noise of the negative ego which discourages, you will hear the voice of the positive ego that encourages.

Shakuntala began to wave her hand in front of her face trying to brush something away. 'Help! Help! This bee is harassing me. It came from the jasmine vine and is attacking me. Someone save me from this bee.'

Dushyanta was amazed at the scene. He began to envy the bee. The bee was brushing intermittently against the fluttering eyelids of the gorgeous damsel. Sometimes it would buzz around the ears of the queenly creature whispering sweet nothings. Sometimes it would taste her lips. Dushyanta was feeling quite desperate at the bee's audacious amorous activities.

Shakuntala ran hither-thither helplessly, trying to get away from the frenzied attack of the intoxicated bee. 'How cruel is this bee! No matter where I go he follows me everywhere. Save this poor girl from this demon,' she cried.

Her amused friends said, 'Neither of us has the capacity to save you now. Only King Dushyanta can save you. Call out to him. Since the whole kingdom is under his protection, surely he will help you.'

Dushyanta smiled at that and felt that this was the perfect opening to make an entrance. While attempting to get away from the troublesome bee, Shankuntala ran towards the mango-jasmine pairing from whence the bee had originated. As she edged closer—

'Who is this foolish demon that troubles a delicate maiden? I am here to protect you divine lady, do not fear.' The abrupt entrance of a handsome stranger caught the girls by surprise.

❧

'What's wrong with you, Shakuntala? Why are you shivering like a leaf in the cold wind?' Standing at the gates of the king's palace, feeling helpless, was the enfeebled Shakuntala. She was wondering how she would deal with her life's greatest decision. A decision much greater and more important than the decision she had taken many years ago. This was a decision that would affect not only her life but two other lives that revolved around her, one of whom was standing right next to her. 'You stand here helplessly, as if you are a stranger to him. Why do you hesitate now? Why do you hesitate to confront your destiny? Are you not confident of the messages of the inner voice that guides you and him? That day you ran towards that mango grove, didn't you know that you were running towards your destiny? When he stepped out of the shadow of that mango tree, didn't you know that your destiny is linked inextricably to his?

'You were so stunned at seeing him that you forgot the codes of hospitality that your father had so painstakingly taught you. You did not offer him water, flowers or fruits, or even sweet words of welcome. You were simply rendered mute. Didn't you make your life's greatest decision while standing there with your head spinning? As your body stood there unmoving, you heard your friends converse with him about you. Seeing your condition, your friends were joking about you right in front of him. They went as far as telling the stranger that Sage Kanva had left a gift for him. While they were laughing at their own joke, the only thing you could manage to whisper to them was to shut their mouths.

'You could hear the stranger asking them the story of your birth. While you wondered why the stranger was interested in your birth, your talkative friends were busy telling him every single detail that he could possibly want to know about you.'

Priyamvada said, 'We are telling you the secret story of her birth, which Sage Kanva himself tells in confidence to the sages who enquire. Many years ago, Sage Vishwamitra was engaged in a series of extreme austerities. Indra, the king of the heavens, became very insecure, suspicious of the intention of the sage in taking up such intense ascetic exercises. He summoned Maneka, the most beautiful of the celestials, and gave her the contract of seducing the sage. Maneka sought help from the celestials to create an ambience where her charms would work to maximum effect and managed to distract Vishwamitra from his asceticism for several years. The result was the birth of Shakuntala. On giving birth to this beautiful girl, Maneka abandoned the delicate baby on the banks of the Malini River and went back to her life of carefree joy in the heavens. Taking pity on that helpless baby, a group of Shakunta birds surrounded her and took turns in caring for and protecting the child in the forest.'

❁ *When we see humans behaving like animals and animals acting compassionate, it feels that humanity has not disappeared, but has simply been transferred from the cities to the forests.*

'The next day, when Sage Kanva visited the river bank to offer his daily prayers, he witnessed the unique scene of a flock of birds absorbed in protecting a human child. Walking up to the peacefully sleeping child, he picked her up and brought her home. Because she was protected by the Shakunta birds, the sage decided to name her Shakuntala. According to Maharishi Kanva, who is a great authority on Vedic scriptures, three kinds of people are considered fathers. The one who gives life, the one who protects life and the one who nourishes life. Vishwamitra gave life, the birds gave protection and Sage Kanva nourished her all her life.'

✿ *Before any ability is given, a responsibility is given.*

'You heard Priyamvada conclude the story by saying that you had three fathers. What shocked you was the stranger's reaction. He expressed great joy on hearing that you were the daughter of Vishwamitra, a former king in whose veins runs the royal blood of the ksatriyas. He went on to appreciate the fact that a human is best guided by the inner voice of the paramatma within. He said that the moment he set his eyes on you, his heart began to yearn to unite with you. But he couldn't think of uniting with the daughter of a brahmana sage. Which is the reason he had been inquiring about your birth, to ascertain your origins. He knew that his inner voice couldn't be wrong. If he was so madly attracted to a girl, she had to be of a compatible background. According to the story he had just heard, you were not just compatible but an ideal match for him. When he began to appreciate the beauty of your eyes, which he compared to that of an antelope, you felt yourself melting in delighted bashfulness. There was something about his voice. You felt like rushing into his arms to hear his voice from closer quarters. You wanted him to whisper all those loving things he was saying about your beauty to your friends, into your ears alone.

'Just as he was about to say something, moving closer to you, a commotion began. The inmates of the ashram pulled him away from you to help them deal with an elephant attack. Wild elephants had entered the ashram premises maddened by fear of the king's hunters and were wrecking not only the ashram but also your heart by interrupting the conversation that was building up.

'As the stranger walked away, your friends pulled you away too. But on the pretext of pulling out an imaginary thorn pricking your feet, you stood there looking at him leaving. Your body was moving in one direction physically but your gaze continued to wander in the opposite direction. You knew that as he moved away physically, he was mentally getting more and more drawn to you.'

❁ *Love is like wearing a seat belt, it has to click first and then you know it works well if it pulls you back forcibly when you push it away.*

'And now you stand here in confusion once again. You can't decide whether you should be moving in his direction or away. When will you finally overcome this confusion and be decisive in the way you were the next day you met him?'

'Will you marry me?'

That one question swept the ground from under her feet. She was dumbfounded. Though she was madly attracted to him, she was least prepared for this. He had managed to find her even in her favourite secret spot, all thanks to her talkative friends. She was seated on a flat rock strewn with the petals of pink lotuses.

This was where she came when she was especially happy or sad. This rock was like a mother on whose lap she sought solace and answers. She had been sitting on the rock since daybreak, trying to figure out the answer to the question her heart had kept asking her since the previous day. A question he had just verbalised in such a straightforward manner.

'Know me to be King Dushyanta. Since you also have royal blood flowing through your veins, I am doing the right thing by proposing to you. Please accept me.' King Dushyanta was on his knees looking into Shakuntala's eyes.

Gathering her composure, Shakuntala said, 'This is not possible. Trying to do the impossible will only bring misery into our lives. I cannot make any decisions myself since I depend on my father to make every decision in my life.'

'But the role of a father is to protect you, not control you. Those who are controlled cannot decide. But those who are protected well are trained enough and capable enough to make their own decisions, based on sound judgement. Since you are protected, not controlled, you can take your own decisions. If you say that due to your love for your father you want him to take this decision, then it is fine. But don't say that because you are dependent on him, he should take your decisions. At the end, it's your decision. It's your heart, your intelligence and your life. Use your connection with your inner voice and ask yourself this question. Ask your inner voice if taking this decision on your own is wrong. Ask your inner voice if this decision is against the path of dharma,' Dushyanta entreated.

❁ *Good decisions are taken when there is alignment between what you want to do and why you want to do it.*

Shakuntala said, 'What you are saying is correct, but I want to leave this decision to my father due to my love and respect for him.'

'Though such sentiments are admirable, I still want you to decide if you want to accept me or reject me based on what your inner voice says. The inner voice is our eternal associate, our only shelter. The inner voice is one's true friend and the inner voice is our real father. When someone is capable of listening to the inner voice, such a person should take the most important decisions of their life by tuning into the message of the inner voice. Ask yourself honestly, are you not attracted to me? When your mind, intelligence and ego love me intensely, how can your decision be wrong? Don't you know that in Vedic culture, the highest form of marriage is a gandharva marriage or love marriage?'

❁ *Trusting yourself means seeing the invisible, experiencing the intangible and understanding the inconceivable nature of faith in oneself and the divine within.*

Shakuntala listened to Dushyanta's words intently and said, 'If the principle of love marriage is approved by the higher authorities and if you are confident that we are capable of making our own decisions, by listening to the directions of the inner voice, then I am definitely ready to marry you. But I have a condition for the marriage to take place.'

Dushyanta was surprised by her speaking about conditions in love. He asked her why they needed conditions if this was true love. She explained that most people in this world act selfishly in love but that in her apparent selfishness there was selfless love. When there is no clarity in love, then it becomes imaginary. Anything imaginary is not true. What is not true is an illusion. Anything that makes us live in illusion brings us misery. The thing that makes us miserable forces us to lose our peace of mind. Where there is loss of peace there is violence. Where there is violence there can be no stable relationship. And where there is no stable relationship there is only struggle. Therefore she explained that he needed to understand her reasoning and agree to her condition before she agreed to marry him.

❁ *In selfishness there can be selfless love and in selflessness there can be selfish interests.*

Highly impressed with Shankuntala's deep, meditative thoughts on love, Dushyanta agreed to abide by her condition. He told her that he had understood that she was highly educated and intelligent. He explained that he had great confidence in her discernment and he knew she would only ask for something that was logical and reasonable. He concluded by saying that whatever she asked would definitely be the right thing.

With a serious demeanour Shakuntala said, 'O King, I will marry you on the condition that the boy born from my womb through you should become the next king.'

Dushyanta began to laugh. He asked her, 'How can I avow this for someone who is not even born? Isn't this unreasonable? He has not even been conceived and you have already made him the king and are expecting me to accept him as such as well.'

❁ *Even before a relationship is born, unreasonable conditions give birth to doubt.*

'This is not some imaginary desire. I am the daughter of a king. I am not only qualified due to my royal pedigree, but also because I have prepared myself through intense austerities to receive the most qualified soul into my womb to create a powerful impact on this world. If due to some act of destiny what I am hoping for doesn't happen, we can discuss alternatives at that point. But till then I want you to take the vow that the boy who will be born to me and you will be the future king,' Shakuntala reasoned.

Agreeing to her reasoning, King Dushyanta married Shakuntala, keeping the inner voice as their primary witness and the deities controlling the elements as their secondary witness. They were united and experienced the most wonderful time of their lives in each other's company. Soon Dushyanta departed to his capital, promising to welcome her shortly to his palace with a royal reception.

❁ *Sometimes it's best to trust God who speaks through our inner instincts rather than trust our intelligence which speaks through our reason.*

~

'When there was no fear then, why is there so much fear now? When there was no guilt then, why is there so much guilt now? Are you fearful of facing reality? Are you guilty of letting down your father or yourself?'

❁ *The fear of reality and the reality of fear, both are equally terrifying.*

'When the king left the ashram, leaving only his promises and his seed in your womb, your father Kanva returned. When you did not go to receive him joyfully like you had always done, he knew something had gone wrong. Without you having to explain anything, he understood everything through his yogic vision, the inner vision that helped him comprehend the past, understand the present and prepare for the future. He saw that the innocent bliss of your childhood had gone, replaced by the guilty misery of adulthood.'

❁ *Innocence bequeaths clarity, while guilt bequeaths obscurity.*

'When he learnt the facts, instead of being upset and disappointed with you, he chose to appreciate your decision and respect your choice. He told you that by choosing to marry a great king like Dushyanta and asking for your son to be the next king, you had brought honour upon your royal lineage. He spoke highly encouraging words and in fact blessed you, saying you will have a son who would rule the world justly. Those words of acceptance from your father who was such a powerful sage encouraged you to believe in the correctness of the choice that you had made and acted as a soothing balm over the wounds of guilt that you were inflicting on yourself.'

❁ *Words of acceptance act as a salve for the wounds of guilt.*

'After receiving such blessings from your father, why are you shivering like a leaf? Why don't you enter the palace and claim what is rightfully yours? Have you lost faith in that inner voice that guided you when you took this decision? Even if you don't have faith in yourself, why don't you seem to have faith in the promises of your husband or even the prophetic words of the sage?

'Are you thinking that the promises may be true and the prophecy may be true, but all that was six years ago? In the last six years, in which every single day seemed to be as long as a year, you seemed to have aged a decade. The wait seemed endless. Every evening ended with you staring in the direction your hope had gone that day, along with King Dushyanta. The only thing that made these six years bearable was your son. A child makes a mother. And what a child he is! Beautiful features with a broad forehead, tender limbs that are strong as iron, with rows of pearly teeth and dark flowing hair. He grew much faster than regular children. At six years of age he is so powerful that he can defeat tigers, boars and even elephants. He would easily overpower these wild beasts and tame them. Sometimes, he would tie them up to trees or the pillars of the hermitage. At other times he would enter the hermitage riding on them proudly. The ashram inmates would be greatly frightened on seeing these wild animals being brought into the precincts of the ashram. Rightly was he named Sarvadamana, the one who conquers everyone.

'The unbelievable strength of your growing son forced Sage Kanva to speak to you about something that had been haunting him. Without mincing words he told you that your son needed his father, that his energy had to be channelled in the right direction. He explained gently that this wouldn't be possible in the ashram. He told you to go and face what you had been avoiding for so long. He told you that you would always remain his daughter, but now you had to take on the role of a wife. Encouraged by your father, who was ever your well-wisher, you decided to make the journey and face your fears. Now as you stand before the gates of the king's courtroom, why are you afraid to face your fears? If not now, when will you do it?'

 *Fear, when not faced, appears stronger.*

'The step that you are about to take to enter the threshold of the royal court will be the most courageous one you have ever taken. Perhaps only less courageous than listening to your inner voice and taking that decision on your own that day.'

'Who are you? Why are you claiming to be my wife? Whose child is this boy whom you claim is my son? Your motive seems to be to bring me infamy and falsely claim rights over the throne for your son. How can I believe you when I don't even recognise you?' Dushyanta spoke with an indifference that brought a chill down Shakuntala's spine. She fell to the ground unable to stand any more. She couldn't believe what she had heard. With trembling lips and fiery rage she thought, 'Was this the person who made all those promises when you last met him? Was this the person you had fallen in love with? How can he be so cruel?

'But what is this? Even now your inner voice is telling you that there must be a logical explanation for his apparently wrong intentions.'

Regaining her stability she decided to face the situation.

'O King, you know everything, yet you are acting like an ordinary man who doesn't hesitate to lie for his personal benefit. Ask your heart where your inner voice resides. Touch your heart and tell the truth. You are trying to hide from your true identity.' Shakuntala was trembling in anger as she spoke these words.

Dushyanta was completely unmoved by her emotions. 'If anyone walks into this court and claims that she is my wife, should I just accept it?'

'Do not doubt his intentions,' her inner voice was telling her. 'Even if there is something wrong in his actions, do not doubt his intentions. Once intentions are in doubt, the relationship is lost forever. Challenge his actions, but do not doubt his intentions.'

❁ *While wrong actions create doubt, good intentions reveal reality.*

'Do you think there was no witness to your commitment? Why are you forgetting that your inner voice is the greatest witness? Your conscience is so close to your heart but still you choose not to see it. Where are your ethics? We had taken our vows with our inner voice as witness but also had the sun, the moon, air, sky, earth, day and night, as witnesses. Those who do not regard all this and still choose the path of lies have no future. Do not reject me. If you disrespect me, then it will be a great blot on your character. Don't pollute your conscience. If you reject me, all prosperity will reject you. All the deities will reject you,' Shakuntala argued.

❁ *A sleeping conscience is the cause of prosperity slipping away. Building trust in others is like mixing water in cement; it takes time to mix it well, but when done it lasts for a lifetime.*

'Do you not remember me? I am the daughter of Vishwamitra and Maneka. I was raised by Sage Kanva. I am your wife. A wife is a man's best friend. A wife completes a man. A man without a wife is like an empty room. A wife plays three roles in a husband's life. In privacy she speaks sweet words of love, in actions of dharma the wife becomes a worthy associate and during crises she is like a mother who helps deal with pain. A man can experience peace even in the most painful situations of life if he is accompanied by his wife. A man who has a wife can be trusted more than a man who is a loner. A husband has to respect his wife as he respects his mother because she becomes the mother of his child. Motherhood has to be respected. The son becomes a manifestation of a man's deepest being. When you see your son standing in front of you, don't you experience yourself as you see him? Just as a person experiences himself while facing a mirror, a father experiences himself when he faces his son. How can you not accept him as your son? What could be a bigger happiness for a father than touching his son's face? The pleasure of touching one's own son is more pleasurable then touching sandalwood paste. If you touch him, you won't need any more proof. A crow takes care of even the eggs of the cuckoo, considering them to be her own. With you being such a powerful king, why wouldn't you want to take responsibility for your own son? Look at how beautiful your son is. Don't you feel like touching him lovingly?'

❁ *You may 'fall' in love if you can 'rise' in responsibility.*

Dushyanta said, 'I have no idea who you are. I cannot understand why you are behaving in such a distasteful manner in front of everyone. Go away! Go wherever you please. You have been rejected by your lusty father Vishwamitra and your mother Maneka. If your birth parents rejected you, how do you expect me to accept you?'

Shakuntala burst out in anger: 'O king, you are able to find fault in everyone but yourself. You can so clearly perceive such faults in others that are as small as a mustard seed, while you are unable to perceive your own fault that is as big as a bilva fruit. Dushyanta, know that my birth is far superior to yours. Born to a celebrated saptarishi and a celestial apsara, I am of divine origin. I have never known what it is to sin, as I was raised in the protected ashram of Sage Kanva.

'An ugly man considers himself more handsome than others only until he looks at himself in the mirror. A really handsome person never vilifies others. A pig always looks for filthy things to eat even when roaming in a beautiful garden. But a goose is an expert in extracting milk even when it is mixed in water. An honest man feels great pain in speaking ill of others, whereas a wicked person derives great pleasure in mocking others. An honest man offers respect to others while a fool abuses everyone around. An honest person never retaliates even when he is injured by the wicked, who derive great pleasure in torturing him. What could be a more ridiculous thing than a wicked person calling an honest person wicked?'

❁ *Before negativity comes out of the mouth, it circulates in every nerve of the brain as pessimism. Then after it comes out of the mouth, it goes back into every nerve of the brain and circulates as guilt.*

'Don't be a hypocrite, O king! Making a water tank is more meritorious than making a hundred wells. Performing a sacrifice is more meritorious than making a hundred water tanks. Begetting a son is more meritorious than performing a sacrifice. But speaking the truth is more meritorious than begetting a hundred sons. If you weigh the merit of performing a thousand horse sacrifices and compare it on a scale with the merit of speaking a single truth, the truth would outweigh the thousand sacrifices. Speaking the truth is equivalent to studying all the Vedas. There is nothing superior to the truth and nothing inferior to falsehood. Those who speak the truth are considered to be in sync with their inner voice.'

❁ *While telling a lie requires intelligence, speaking the truth requires guts.*

'O king, speak the truth. If you choose to embrace falsehood, then I do not want to associate with such a person. I will walk away from your life this very moment. In fact, I would say that no one should associate with you if you choose a life of falsehood.'

Shakuntala was at her wits' end. She had no energy left to dispute further. An argument began with her inner voice, 'Should I still listen to my inner voice and not doubt his intentions? How can I continue to not doubt his intentions? My inner voice seems to be misguiding me.'

There was tumult in the court. 'This is your son, Dushyanta! This is your wife, Dushyanta! Accept them!' The whole court rose and spoke in unison. 'Our inner voice is telling us that this pure lady is definitely telling the truth. There is such depth to what she says, such purity in her words. She has to be true.'

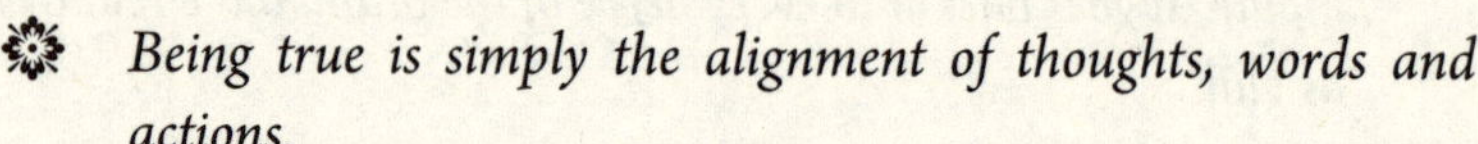

Being true is simply the alignment of thoughts, words and actions.

Seeing the whole court rise and express their opinion in unison, Dushyanta smiled and stood up from his throne. Suddenly a disembodied voice echoed in the court. 'Shakuntala is your wife Dushyanta and Sarvadamana is your son! Accept them and become fortunate. Your son will rule the world and will be celebrated by the name Bharata.'

Dushyanta walked up to Shankuntala and fell at her feet. Touching her feet he begged for forgiveness for acting so cruelly and not being a good husband and father. He explained that since he was a king and their union took place privately, he thought that people would think that their union was based on lust and would not accept the sanctity of it. He said, 'Even if I accepted you and our son immediately, people would have doubted our son's birth and he would have to face tremendous criticism in the future. All this while I have been contemplating how to establish the purity of our relationship and at the same time ensure that our son never has to face any criticism in the future. Let me assure you that never for one moment in all this while have I forgotten you and my intense love for you. While I am very well aware of my roles and responsibilities as a husband and father, my primary role of being king made me behave in this way. In such a highly responsible position, I needed to ensure that there was no blot or infamy associated with our family. To ensure long-term peace, I caused temporary anxiety in your life, my dear. Please forgive me for the ill means that I adopted. I assure you that for the rest of my life, I will worship you and our son. I will ensure that you never face a single difficulty in your life from today onwards.'

 *Anxiety and peace are inversely proportionate.*

When you want peace in the short-term, you get anxiety in the long-term. But when you take up something that gives you short-term anxiety, you end up with long-term peace.

With great respect and care Dushyanta addressed Shakuntala. As she considered the points that he was making, while explaining his misdeeds, Shakuntala could understand the reasoning for his apparently wrong actions. Slowly, the old sensitive Dushyanta began to emerge from inside the insensitive one. Shakuntala began to feel the same warmth she had experienced the first day she was with him. As she looked into his eyes while he was kneeling, touching her feet, she could perceive his sincerity. At that moment, Shakuntala decided to heed her inner voice that was telling her to rededicate herself to him. She decided to trust life once again.

 *We tend to trust ourselves so much to make life work that we tend to forget to trust life, which tends to work itself out perfectly.*

Dushyanta crowned his son Sarvadamana the heir to the throne. Eventually, his son became such a powerful king that the entire subcontinent owed him allegiance. In keeping with his power and influence, he was bequeathed various names. The chief of them being Sarvabhauma and Bharata. The name Bharata stuck and eventually he came to be known by that name. Bharata became an emperor in the true sense and was so famous that the entire territory was named after him. The result of two people who tuned into their inner voice was someone who gave a voice to an entire civilisation.

 *When you tune into your inner voice, the world tunes into your outer voice.*

TRUSTING RELATIONSHIPS

Sometimes called the 'gut', sometimes 'intuition', sometimes 'our connection with the paramatma', sometimes 'inner voice' and, most commonly, 'trust'. Trust is the foundation on which relationships thrive. Without trust they only strive. Trust is the highest tribute one can offer any relationship. But as they say, the real test of a ship is not how good it looks at the dock but how well it does in a storm. The trust factor gets heavily tested in the midst of the storms of doubt, not during the initial fair weather of love.

The story of Shakuntala and Dushyanta is a story of trust. This tale explores a seldom discussed aspect that is nevertheless very important for lasting relationships, especially when there is doubt created due to circumstances. It's a story in which two people allowed their inner voice to guide them into trusting one another even in the midst of the greatest storm of doubt.

Trusting another is easy when there is a good track record of reliability. Building trust in others is like making cement: it takes time to mix it well, but when done it lasts a lifetime in the form of concrete. It takes a sustained amount of time, effort and constancy to build strong muscles of trust. But it simply takes one strong instance of doubt to tear people apart. Unfortunately, in relationships people often embark upon self-created doubting sessions. Even when there is no reason to doubt their partner, they do so. Even before a relationship is born, unreasonable conditions give birth to doubt. As the pendulum of a relationship swings between trust and doubt, love is lost and replaced by detestation.

Shakuntala's circumstances pushed her to doubt her decision of listening to her inner voice and trusting Dushyanta. Every bit of evidence pointed to the magnitude of her mistake in marrying him. Her father, her friends, Dushyanta's behaviour and even her own intelligence were telling her that the relationship was over. But there was that one little voice within her that was whispering into her ears to not give up her faith. Though feeble, it still existed. That inner voice inspired her to not give up on this pivotal relationship and have faith that there must be some reason that would eventually explain everything.

Where there is love, there has to be trust. Loving someone is giving them the power to break your heart, but trusting them not to. Marriage is not just about two people living together, but about two people trusting one another. The process of trusting another begins by trusting oneself first. Trusting oneself means seeing the invisible, experiencing the intangible and understanding the inconceivable nature of faith in oneself and the divine within. One should learn to trust oneself because one's perceptions are far more accurate than one is willing to believe. Each one of us is guided by an inner voice whose role is to bring joy into our lives. But we tend to be so engrossed in the noise generated by the negative ego which discourages that we lose the ability to hear the voice of the positive ego that encourages. Trust becomes much easier if we filter out the discouraging noise of the negative ego and give centre stage to the encouraging sounds of the positive ego. The negative ego convinces you that your needs won't be met in your relationship, which then manifests itself as anger, anxiety, frustration, suspicion and lack of confidence.

Shakuntala was convinced that her inner voice would not misguide her. She had made her choice and she wanted to trust that choice. She realised that if she had made her initial choice inspired by her inner perceptions, then it couldn't be so wrong.

In life, most decisions we make are governed by reason. However, when it comes to relationships, we need to trust God who speaks through our inner instincts rather than purely trusting our intelligence, which only speaks the language of reason. Just as a child has the deepest relationships because it has complete trust in them, we need to rediscover the lost child in us. We tend to trust ourselves so much to make life work that we forget to trust life, which finds a way to work itself out. Rather than believing in intelligence only, learn to believe in life. When you learn to have faith in yourself, God and life, you will learn to trust others as well.

While Shakuntala was learning to trust herself and God by relying on her inner voice, Dushyanta was being crushed between the responsibility of being a king and that of a husband. He was hoping and praying that Shakuntala would not misunderstand his actions as stemming from the wrong intentions. Life had put him in a tricky situation. Though he yearned to be with the person he loved more than life, he was conflicted due to his commitment to his responsibilities as a king, on which millions of people depended. He wanted Shakuntala to be accepted as his wife with everyone's blessing and not with any friction. He knew that if their son was to become the next king, then the acceptance of their relationship publicaly had to be a smooth one. To bring about long-term stability, he had to cause short-term disruption in Shakuntala's life. He was hoping that her reliance on her inner voice and on him would not wane before they received wholehearted support from the citizens of his kingdom. When Shakuntala learnt to trust herself, God and life, she ended up learning to trust Dushyanta as well.

Chapter 4

THE OTHER BEFORE ONESELF

Looks like adventure runs in their blood! Those who thought that the adventures of Arjuna were the most exciting ones ought to hear the story of Udayana, a descendent of Arjuna. His adventures are as good if not better. Born six generations after Arjuna, his adventures began even before his birth.

King Janamejaya, the great grandson of Arjuna, had a son called Satanika. Satanika was married to Vishnumati. The couple remained childless for a long time till King Satanika met Sandilya Rishi in the forest, through whose blessings they were favoured with a son they named Sahasranika. King Satanika was such a valorous warrior that he would often receive invitations from the gods to lead battles on their behalf. King Satanika was killed in one such fierce skirmish. Subsequently, Sahasranika was declared his successor. The invitations from the heavens continued even during the reign of King Sahasranika. On one such heavenly trip, Indra, the king of the devatas, took him for a stroll in the renowned garden, the Nandan Kanan. King Sahasranika caught sight of a celestial couple absorbed in romantic play in the garden. That scene triggered his own desires and he became lost in a world of yearnings. Perceiving the sudden change in the king's behaviour, Indra empathised with the unmarried king and revealed to him that he would find love with an extremely beautiful girl named Mrighavati very soon. Their love was one that would continue from a previous birth. In his previous life, King Sahasranika had been a Vasu named Vidhuma and Mrighavati had been an apsara named Alambusa. They had fallen in love at first sight. In fact, this meeting had happened right in front of Lord Brahma. Both were so absorbed in each other that they completely forgot Brahma's presence. Angry at this disrespect, Lord Brahma uttered a curse that sentenced them to be born on earth. Revealing this story, Indra assured Sahasranika that very soon he would be reunited with his love.

❁ *Absorption that leads to sensitivity is called empathy.*
Absorption that leads to neglect is called apathy.

From the moment Indra uttered the word 'Mrighavati', King Sahasranika became engaged in imagining her beauty. He wasn't aware of getting into his chariot or of the chariot reaching half way between heaven and earth. Nor was he aware that the most beautiful of all apsaras, the personal master creation of Lord Brahma, Tilottama, was in the chariot just to spend some private moments with him. While Tilottama was shyly expressing her heartfelt love for him, Sahasranika was flying free in his far-off imaginary world, unable to hear anything she said. After completing her confession of love she turned to him for a reply and saw him staring into space, totally lost. The broken-hearted Tilottama cursed him, saying he would be separated from the person he was thinking of for a period of fourteen years. The king didn't even hear the curse!

In a few days, King Sahasranika's ministers received word

about the whereabouts of a princess named Mrighavati who was still unmarried. Accompanied by a great number of gifts, the king sent a marriage proposal to her father. Soon they were married and Mrighavati conceived within a month. The love between husband and wife grew every day. They focused on fulfilling the other's smallest desire, no matter how trivial it was. One day she expressed a very funny wish to her beloved. She wanted a dip in a pond of red water instead of regular water. That evening, King Sahasranika arranged for red water to be filled in the terrace pond in Mrighavati's private quarters. Wearing only a single piece of cloth, Mrighavati entered the blood red waters of the pond in great joy. Her eyes began to gleam with childish happiness. Her long-standing dream had been fulfilled by her husband in an instant.

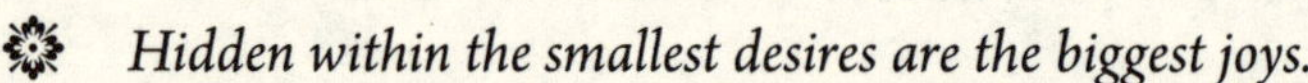

Hidden within the smallest desires are the biggest joys. Small drops of water when collected fill up a water tank. Similarly, when efforts are made to fulfil small desires, it fills up the love tank.

As she was splashing about gleefully, a huge eagle swooped down, picked her up in its claws and flew away. The giant bird dropped her on top of the Mountain of the Rising Sun. When the bird saw that she was alive, and was running around and screaming, it realised it had made a mistake in assuming that what it had picked up was a lump of flesh floating around in a pool of blood. The bird abandoned her on that lonely mountain and flew away. Hours passed as the helpless, pregnant Mrighavati struggled to escape the mountaintop but to no avail. Sleep overtook the delicate lady who was clad in just one piece of cloth. She lay down on the cold rocks of the mountain, slowly drifting off into a dream-like state. She dreamt of a dangerously poisonous snake, a hundred-metre long and as thick as the leg of an elephant, coiling around her legs. In her dream she struggled to escape the vice-like grip of the slithering reptile. Unable to tolerate the nightmare, she struggled to wake up and opened her eyes, only to realise that it wasn't a dream! It was all real! Mrighavati screeched for help, as the huge mouth of the deadly snake inched closer to her face.

 *Some truths appear gentler than dreams but are harsher than reality.*

The next moment, the snake froze! It looked this way and that. Then it loosened its grip on her and slowly slithered away. She got up with great difficulty to see a young renunciate standing in front of her. Observing her helplessness, her clothing and her pregnant state, he gently led her to the ashram of Sage Jamadagni. Jamadagni welcomed her to his hermitage and cared for her like a loving father. She narrated what had happened to her and he assured her that very soon everything would be set right. In a few months, Mrighavati gave birth to a brilliant baby boy. The moment the child was born, an ethereal voice announced that this child would become the most renowned king of his time and would eventually also become the master of the Vidyadharas. Since he was born in Udayadri or the Mountain of the Rising Sun, he would be celebrated as Udayana.

 *Every sun is born in the darkness.*

Under the tutelage of Sage Jamadagni, the intelligent Udayana grew up to be a talented and knowledgeable child. By age fourteen, he became an expert in the martial arts and learned in the scriptures. His strength, combined with his intellect and complemented by his natural humility, made him Sage Jamadagni's favourite disciple. The only symbol of his connection with King Sahasranika was a bracelet that the king had given Mrighavati as a present on their wedding day. The priceless bracelet had the name of the king carved on it in gold. Mrighavati had tied it on Udayana's arm. Every time she embraced her son, she cried as she got reminded of her beloved husband.

One day as Udayana was travelling through the forest while on an errand his guru had given him, he came across a scene that caused him great mental anguish. He saw a huge snake trapped by a man. The snake was struggling to gain its freedom. The pain etched on the snake's face invoked great compassion in Udayana. Walking up to the snake charmer, he ordered him to release the struggling reptile. The surprised man lamented that this snake was his only source of livelihood since the previous snake he owned had died. Udayana immediately took off the bracelet that his mother had given him and handed it over to the man in exchange for the snake's freedom. The man danced away happily, well aware that a truly valuable item had fallen into his hands.

✿ *Everyone wants others to become investors in their happiness. In avoiding investing in others' happiness people show bankruptcy in their happiness accounts.*

When the charmer had left, the snake began to speak to Udayana. He revealed that he was Vasunemi, the older brother of Vasuki, king of snakes. In gratitude for saving him the snake bestowed a few special gifts upon Udayana. The first was a special musical instrument, a lute known as Ghosavati that could produce divinely melodious musical notes. He next bequeathed the art of making garlands which would never fade, followed by the art of creating artistic markings on the forehead, which would never fade. Armed with these special gifts from the celestial snake, Udayana returned to the ashram infinitely richer in knowledge.

❁ *When you give what you have, you gain what you don't have.*

Meanwhile, the snake charmer joyfully walked out of the forest and, after weeks of travel, coincidentally reached the capital of King Sahasranika's kingdom. He then tried to sell the bracelet to some jewellers. The jewellers saw the name of their king engraved on it and raised an alarm. Soon the snake charmer was arrested and produced before the king. The moment his eyes fell on the bracelet, the king let out an anguished cry. This was the same bracelet he had given his beloved on the day of their wedding, fourteen years ago! Catching hold of the snake charmer, the king demanded to know from whom he had procured this bracelet. The snake charmer narrated the incident of how the bracelet had come to him. The king immediately set out on an expedition to the Mountain of the Rising Sun. While he was travelling towards that distant land, a nagging question appeared in his mind. Why had he received no information about his wife for so many years though he had searched far and wide? That's when Matali, the charioteer of Indra, appeared and revealed Tilottama's fourteen-year curse, which had officially ended that day.

❁ *The questions 'what', 'how' and 'when' lead to an answer but the question 'why' only leads to more questions.*

The best way to deal with the whys of life is to wait.

After weeks of travel, they reached Sage Jamadagni's hermitage. Seeing King Sahasranika at his doorstep, the sage welcomed him in with great ceremony. Mrighavati was thrilled to see her husband after more than a decade of separation. Love, sorrow, shyness, joy swept through her like a surging tidal wave as her husband turned and looked at her. She was so confused that she remained immobile. Sage Jamadagni handed over Udayana to his father and informed the king that he had imparted the highest possible education to his son. The king's eyes flooded with tears when he saw his wife and young son. Before leaving the ashram and returning to the palace, Mrighavati offered her heartfelt gratitude to the sage for taking care of her as a father would. The sage in turn blessed the three of them profusely and went back to his duties.

❁ *Emotions never travel alone. When you experience one emotion, there will surely be a few more hanging around.*

The first thing the king did on returning to his kingdom was to officially appoint Udayana the heir to the throne. Udayana gradually became an expert in managing affairs of the state. He had a team of three ministers called Yaugandharayana, Rumanvan and Vasantaka, with whom he worked closely. The four of them could handle any mission, big or small, perfectly. With his son excelling at administration, King Sahasranika stepped back, allowing the young prince more freedom. Finally, when the king felt that Udayana would be able to handle the entire responsibility of kingship, he crowned him the next king. As the crowning ceremony drew to a close, a celestial voice rang out, prophesying that King Udayana would rule the entire planet, assisted ably by his three ministers. The divine ordinance gave Sahasranika enough confidence to leave the kingdom in his son's capable hands and depart on a one-way pilgrimage to the Himalayas with his dear wife Mrighavati.

 *Renunciation is always better than elimination.*

When leaders don't renounce their positions on time, they get eliminated with time.

The glory of King Udayana spread far and wide. He began to be spoken of as one of the most charismatic rulers that had ever ruled on earth. His valour, strength, intelligence, enterprise, scriptural knowledge and musical skills were the talk of every town. Chandamsena, the king of Ujjaini, was eager to have his daughter Vasavadatta marry Udayana. The only problem was that the two kingdoms had been hostile to each other for decades. Chandamsena felt that this alliance would bring many years of rivalry to an end. In order to make this match happen, the king decided to ensure that Udayana fell in love with his daughter. He wrote a letter to Udayana humbly requesting him to come to Ujjaini to give his daughter musical lessons.

However, Udayana replied that if the princess wanted to learn music from him, she should come to the teacher and not expect the teacher to come to her. This insult was too much for Chandamsena to handle and he decided to capture the arrogant king with trickery. Chandamsena possessed a famous elephant called Nadagiri. The elephant was huge. Regular elephants seemed like babies compared to it. The king had a wooden elephant made of the same size as Nadagiri and stationed it in the forested area of the Vindhya mountains, close to Udayana's kingdom. The elephant was made in such a way that from a short distance away it looked exactly like the original. The artificial elephant was hollow within and spacious enough to house many soldiers. In fact, the elephant was a mechanical marvel and could actually move slowly in any direction.

 *Whether it is the Trojan horse or the Nadagiri elephant, the lesson is the same.*

Inside someone unusual is something unusual.

In the darkness of the night, the dummy elephant was stationed in a section of the forest that was regularly monitored by Udayana's soldiers. Once in position, the wait began. There was no movement in the forest most of the next day, except for occasional wild animals trying to figure out what this huge, immobile, unfamiliar animal was. The soldiers inside had fun scaring them away by getting the wooden elephant to make random movements. Come evening, they sensed a group of men approaching the elephant from all directions. All at once the forest was filled with divine music. It was King Udayana playing his famous lute to attract the elephant's attention. He had fallen into the trap. As the king advanced towards the artificial elephant, it began to move backwards. The Ujjaini soldiers cleverly lured the king away from his soldiers. The cover of darkness helped the soldiers hidden inside the elephant to retain their camouflage. When they noticed that they had separated the king from his soldiers, they broke the elephant open and attacked him from all sides. Completely surrounded, King Udayana was forced to surrender.

❁ *While you are busy trapping someone you may already be in a trap.*

In Ujjaini, King Chandamsena welcomed King Udayana with a sarcastic smile. Completely cut off from his kingdom and his people, Udayana had no option but to cooperate with Chandamsena till he found some way out of this sticky situation.

However, Chandamsena made sure Udayana was treated with great respect and care. Except for his desire to communicate with his kingdom and his desire to return to his kingdom, every other desire was taken care of meticulously.

For Udayana, the only good thing about being held captive in this enemy kingdom was the enemy's daughter. Udayana had been instantly attracted to the stunning princess. Vasavadatta too fell madly in love with the charming king. They met for musical lessons every day, but most of their time together flew by in simply staring at each other. Needless to say, neither was ready to admit that they were actually in love with their enemy. Udayana was a great teacher and Vasvadatta loved learning from him. Very soon she became adept at playing the lute and the two would make music together for hours.

❁ *Spending time together is more important than spending a life together.*

Time spent together is saved as memories. A life spent together is saved as dates.

Meanwhile, in Udayana's kingdom, the intelligence network reported to the ministers that their enemy had kidnapped the king using the hollow elephant trick. The three ministers immediately sprung into action. Minister Rumanvan was entrusted with the administration of the kingdom till the king returned. Ministers Yaugandharayana and Vasantaka left for Ujjaini, taking along with them Yogeshwara, who was a brahmarakshasa. But a friendly one!

❁ *Roses have dangerous thorns as friends because soft hands are more dangerous to them than prickly thorns.*

The entrance of a brahmarakshasa in the kingdom sent the citizenry into terror. Disturbed by this, Yogeshwara got angry. Yaugandharayana pacified him somehow and convinced him to remain in invisible mode. Agreeing to his friend's suggestion, the brahmarakshasa Yogeshwara made himself invisible. They could only hear his voice. Acting as their guide and advisor, the first thing he told them was to adopt disguises. Following his advice, Yaugandharayana disguised himself as an old man who was a total crackpot. Vasantaka took the disguise of a sick man who was heavily constipated, due to which he would constantly hold his tummy as if in pain.

As soon as they entered Ujjaini, Yaugandharayana began a series of mad stunts. His comical facial expressions and his silly actions made him an instant hit in the city. People gathered around enjoying the show. He was acting so foolish that children began to follow him everywhere for non-stop free entertainment. Vasantaka acted as if he was the guardian of the mad Yaugandharayana, who he claimed was his cousin. Vasantaka kept asking people for a place where he could answer nature's call comfortably for a few hours. Together, the two created a real sensation in Ujjaini.

As word spread about the duo, the king came to know about them and decided to invite them to his court for some fun. Within fifteen minutes of their 'grand entrance' the king had laughed more than he had in decades. Vasantaka became as famous for his masterful story telling as for his intestinal issues. He could tell a small story for hours or tell a big story in minutes. No matter how much he spoke, people were ready to listen. The king felt so happy in their company that he asked them to be housed in the palace itself.

 *Learning begins at the end of entertainment.*

Udayana recognised them at first glance. Late at night the three met secretly in the palace gardens to formulate their plan. Udayana stated that if he had to leave Ujjaini then it would be along with Princess Vasavadatta. The two ministers tried to explain to him that it would be very risky and it would be difficult to take the princess along, especially if she was not willing. Udayana's smile answered that question. They continued smoothly, saying that even if the princess was willing, it would be a massive security risk for both countries. Kidnapping an enemy princess wasn't an advisable thing to do at all. Udayana turned to leave, indicating that he wasn't asking them for their opinion but giving them an instruction that they had to carry out.

 *Telling is always met by doubt while asking is mostly met by trust.*

Telling is trusting yourself, while asking is trusting relationships over yourself.

Then Udayana paused and said with a backward glance, 'First things first! Let us verify if the princess wants me at all. I haven't expressed my love for her nor has she for me.' He departed, smiling slyly at Vasantaka. That smile meant something that Vasantaka wasn't comfortable with. Udayana always put him in such odd situations. And every time he put Vasantaka in a fix like this, he simply left with that enigmatic smile.

While Udayana slept peacefully, Vasantaka spent the whole night thinking about how he could make Udayana's feelings known to the princess. In the middle of the night, he got an out-of-the-box idea. It was now his turn to smile. As he drifted off to sleep, all the bits and pieces of his idea floated around in his mind. He saw an elephant, he was flying in an eagle, he saw an island, he saw gold, he saw the dome of a temple and he heard a scream…

❁ *A smile on one's face may often create frowns on another.*

A smile that lights up others' faces is like a candle, while a smile that distorts others' faces is like a wildfire.

The next morning Vasavadatta insisted that the two jokers spend some time with her. She wanted to hear Vasantaka's stories. Ever since she had heard about his mastery of storytelling, she had been looking forward to being entertained by some really good stories. She was seated on a soft cushion, all excited to hear the story that Vasantaka had promised would change her life forever. Vasantaka narrated the love story of Lohajanga and Rupinika with utmost drama. Whenever he referred to Lohajanga he looked towards Udayana and whenever he spoke about Rupinika he looked at Vasavadatta. From the very first sentence he had completely arrested Vasavadatta's attention. He began thus—

❁ *Stories can bridge the gap between two hearts.*

Everyone began to shout and scream. 'Goddess Mara is falling! We are dead! We are dead!'

There was utter confusion so early in the morning in the city. The first person who saw the goddess was a beggar who had come to sit at the entrance of the temple to begin his day. He had a habit of looking up at the dome of the temple at the chakra or disc that was mounted on it. He considered looking at the chakra to be as good as looking upon the holy deities in the sanctum sanctorum. He had mechanically looked up at the chakra and done his quick hand gestures and lip movements as part of the prayer ritual he had invented for himself. Just when he sat down to assume his begging duties, he felt something was wrong today. There was something unusual that he had overlooked. He got up and looked up again at the temple dome.

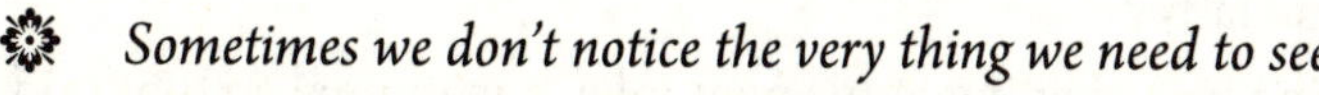

Sometimes we don't notice the very thing we need to see.

He began to scream and run around, announcing, 'Goddess Mara is falling! We are dead! Dead!'

Panic spread and hundreds of people joined in the call. Soon a huge crowd of worried onlookers had gathered around to see the highly disturbing sight on top of the temple dome. Goddess Mara was standing on top of the temple and it seemed like she was about to fall on them. Many of the onlookers were on their knees, fervently praying to the goddess not to fall on them. Many were offering incense, flowers and lamps to her in order to pacify her.

Completely nude except for the charcoal black paint covering the front portion of her body and red oil paint covering the back, the goddess stood on a plate that was placed on top of the dome. She was holding on to the pole that held up the chakra. Adorned with a garland of bones and skulls, she seemed to be death personified. Her head was shaved at five places and she sported five untidy tufts of hair, which gave her a truly ghastly appearance. She seemed to be screaming at the top of her voice but what she was saying was muffled by the thousands of voices of the onlookers. Everyone assumed that she was warning them that she would fall soon, which would mark the end of creation.

When that rumour spread, their fervour reached fever-pitch as they prayed to her desperately, begging her not to fall.

❁ *While someone may be pleading, you are busy concluding. Assuming without knowing is like walking backwards while expecting to go forward.*

A young boy commented, 'Doesn't she look like Makaradarshtra, the cruel lady?'

As he was giggling at his own joke, a man next to him said, 'That's right. It looks exactly like her.' The man also began to giggle, thinking about the irony. In fact he began to imagine how Makaradarshtra would have looked mounted on the plate. Then he realised that he didn't have to imagine the scene, he just had to look up. That's exactly how she would look. Soon the giggling became contagious and all the onlookers started giggling.

Finally one of them cried out, 'Look she is about to fall!'

That's when they all noticed that her hands were trembling and she was about to fall off the plate. As a hush fell over the crowd, they realised that all this while she had been pleading with them to help her get off the plate. The King was immediately informed about the emergency and he sent the army to the rescue straight away.

When Makaradarshtra was finally clothed, rescued and brought to the king, the king asked her to explain how she had reached there. She told him something shocking. Her statement was that Lord Vishnu had dropped her on top of that plate on the temple spire. The king began to laugh loudly telling her that she was hallucinating. He told her to give him a more believable explanation. When she kept saying the same thing over and over again, the king lost his patience. She screamed that Lord

Vishnu had indeed come on his Garuda carrier, carrying the four emblems of shanka, chakra, gada and padma in his hands. He put her on his bird carrier and dropped her there. The king got her sent home declaring that she was mad.

❁ *Often the truth appears exactly like madness.*

As soon as she left, the king walked to his inner chambers, where someone was waiting for him.

When he saw a stranger seated in his private bedroom, the king was taken aback and held his sword aloft in self-defence. The next moment the king relaxed, as the stranger bowed in reverence. 'What are you doing in my private chambers? How did you manage to get in despite such tight security?'

The stranger smiled strangely and pointing to the huge open veranda, he said, 'I flew in from there.'

The king walked to the balcony and looked down and realised that it was impossible for a mere human to have scaled that wall. The king looked at the stranger for an explanation. Instead of explaining anything, the stranger pointed to the table. On it were four of the most sparkling golden objects the king had ever seen. This was the purest form of gold that he had ever seen in his life. Inspecting them from closer quarters, the king realised that the four symbols of Lord Vishnu were lying on his table. The king looked at the stranger in puzzlement.

❁ *Whilst we are busy looking for answers through open doors, they fly in silently through the open windows of life.*

The stranger requested the king to take a seat and allow him to explain everything in detail. Introducing himself as Lohajanga, the stranger began his story. He warned the king that this would be the strangest story he had ever heard and if at the end of the story the king didn't believe anything then he wouldn't be surprised. But he felt it was his duty to furnish the king with an explanation.

He said that a month ago he had gone to visit a remote temple, far away from the city. That's where he saw that angel for the first time. She was so beautiful that he forgot to breathe. Her name was Rupinika. After seeing her beauty, everyone would agree there was no better name for her than that. He was supposed to be in the temple for just a few minutes and then he had other pressing duties to attend to. But as soon as he saw her, his life seemed to freeze from that very moment. Lohajanga spent the rest of the day simply following her about, almost without conscious volition. Initially, Rupinika did not notice the handsome man following her. But when her friends pointed him out, she began to notice him. Of course she didn't want him to know that she was also looking at him. She made sure to look in his direction only when he had turned away for a few moments. She also purposely delayed her return and the two of them spent most of the day playing silent games. By the end of the day, both were madly in love with each other.

❁ *Love is a silent game that two pair of eyes play with each other.*

When she returned home, Lohajanga followed her to the entrance of her house. He got the shock of his life when he recognised the house she entered. This was the house of the wiliest woman in the city. Makaradarshtra, the owner of the house, was not just a courtesan but was also considered one of the most cruel women in the kingdom. Her arrogance, pride and her influence over the most powerful men in the kingdom was well known. She had a flock of courtesans under her wing. Literally every rich, influential and aristocratic man in the city had visited her at some time or the other. She knew too many secrets and was too dangerous to be taken lightly. Lohajanga was highly confused when this beautiful and pious girl walked into such an infamous place.

❁ *Sometimes the worst and the best reside together like a lotus in muck or like heads and tails.*

On inquiring further, Lohajanga discovered that Rupinika was Makaradarshtra's daughter and her nature was exactly the opposite of her mother's. Though she lived in such an abominable place, Rupinika had remained highly pious and pure. Lohajanga also learnt that of late, her mother had been pushing her against her will to take up the oldest profession in the world to continue her legacy. So far Rupinika's age had been the factor that had saved her but soon she would no longer be able to refuse her mother. In fact many unscrupulous men had been eyeing her, including some highly influential men in the king's court.

Understanding that time was of the essence, Lohajanga became bolder in his approach. Very soon he directly confronted Rupinika and expressed the state of his heart to her. Rupinika acknowledged her attraction to him, but also revealed her awkward situation. Lohajanga promised her that he would take her away from this murky situation very soon. Though she appreciated his love and affection for her, she wondered how he would manage to counter her mother's influence and power over the aristocracy. Nonetheless she decided to live for the moment and enjoy every loving minute she spent with this gentle soul.

Their love increased exponentially every day. Every meeting only increased their longing for each other. Of course they tried to keep their meetings as discreet as possible, but how long could they keep it hidden from the shrewd eyes of Makaradarshtra?

❁ *Someone who has time for you even in quicksand will surely have time for you while standing on strong land.*

One day Makaradarshtra chanced upon Lohajanga jumping across the gate of her house in the middle of the night. She confronted her daughter who eventually gave in and told her everything. Makaradarshtra began to lecture her about how their profession and the business of love go ill together. She began to educate her about how a courtesan could never have feelings or sentiments in her heart. She went on to say that being a courtesan is like taking sanyas or having detachment from all attachments.

❁ *Attachment and detachment are twins that look alike but have completely different natures.*

Rupinika once again pleaded with her mother that she had no desire to become a courtesan and would like to live a householder's life with Lohajanga. Her mother slapped her and explained that she had raised her with so much love and affection only so she could take over the successful establishment that she had created. Rupinika argued so much that her mother hit her and walked away. She warned her daughter against ever meeting her lover again.

Despite her mother's warning, Rupinika couldn't resist meeting Lohajanga. When Makaradarshtra saw Lohajanga entering her house again to meet Rupinika, she immediately went to the prince and informed him about the whole love affair. Now the prince had his eyes on Rupinika and had already told

Makaradarshtra that he wanted to be the first person to be with her when she made her entry into the profession. Reminding the prince of his desire, Makaradarshtra encouraged the prince to act immediately. Being prodded in this way, the prince sent an envoy of soldiers to take care of Rupinika's lover. He told his men to be discreet about it so that no one should get even an inkling that the assault has been initiated by the prince.

Lohajanga and Rupinika were lost into each other, unaware that the house was being encircled by armed men who were trained to kill. At the first strike, Lohajanga ducked just in time, to pick up a ring that had fallen and the sword swung inches from his head. Instantly, Lohajanga pushed the swordsman away and jumped out of the window of Rupinika's bedroom. A wild chase began as Lohajanga somehow tricked, pushed and beat a few of the armed men surrounding the house. He began to run pell-mell down the streets of the city, closely pursued by the armed soldiers. They finally managed to outrun him and surrounded him on all sides. Beating him black and blue, they warned him against coming back into the city. They bundled up his badly bruised body and threw him into the excrement pit on the outskirts of the city.

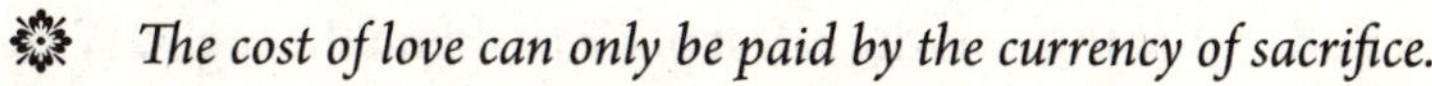

The cost of love can only be paid by the currency of sacrifice.

For hours, Lohajanga lay in that filth with absolutely no strength to get up. Finally at sunset, he mustered some energy to get up. He had no courage left to go back into the city. At the other end of the excrement pit was a forest and he knew that the river flowed close by. He wanted to get rid of all the filth and find a safe place to spend the night, so he staggered in that direction. Walking through the muck was an ordeal, but it was better than lying in it and it was much better than being in a city with filthy people. During the tussle that had taken place, Lohajanga had gotten hold of a bracelet that only the men of the king's army wore on their arms. He was disappointed to learn that the royal palace was involved so intimately with a house of ill repute. He understood that Makaradarshtra had got to know about her daughter's love affair with him and would have used her influence to get rid of him.

❁ *Filthy roads are better than filthy minds; at least their filth is visible.*

Finally reaching the river, Lohajanga washed himself and began to look for a safe spot to spend the night. By then it had become dark and he could hear wild animals prowling in the vicinity. He began to tremble. Following the river, he kept walking deeper into the forest. Then he saw a very strange scene. A carcass of a huge elephant was lying adjacent to the river and about five or six jackals were exiting it from the rear. When they came out through the hole they had made, he realised that the elephant was hollow from within. The predators had eaten away all the parts inside the elephant and had left the elephant's thick hide and bones untouched. Once the jackals had left, Lohajanga concluded that this was the safest place to spend the night. With great difficulty he pushed himself through the narrow opening and settled down for the night in the spacious inner chamber within the body of the elephant. He managed to seal the entry point from within for safety.

❁ *Smaller entities make their living inside bigger entities.*

Small humans who are uncomfortable with themselves prefer to hide under the glamour and success of bigger humans.

Exhaustion took over and he drifted into a deep sleep despite his surroundings. He had a dream that he was on a boat that was floating on water. All through the night the dream continued and he felt he was seated in a boat that was rocking in the waves of an ocean.

Many hours later, from above him he heard a tapping sound. Who was knocking on the door? He got up, assuming that he was in his bed but when he tried to sit up, his head banged against the rib cage of the elephant. That's when he recalled that he had slept inside a dead elephant in the middle of a forest. Trying to avoid any hasty actions, he waited to find out who was pecking at the elephant from the outside. In a few minutes the pecking stopped and he could hear a tearing sound and glaring light flooded the cavity, blinding Lohaganja for an instant. Then a pair of yellow eyes met Lohajanga's for a few seconds. It dawned on him that he was staring into the eyes of a giant vulture. He screamed at the top of his lungs. That scream scared the bird so much that it pulled its head away and shrieked at the top of its voice. The next moment it flapped its wings and flew away. Lohajanga stood up and peeked out, expecting to see the river and the forest scene that he had seen the previous evening. But what he saw shocked him beyond comprehension. He had no idea how he had reached the middle of a vast ocean. In every direction he saw, there was only water, there was not even a remote hint of land anywhere. That's when he realised that the dream of floating on water hadn't been a dream after all. He concluded that the river must have flooded overnight and as a result the carcass of the elephant was carried away by the river into the ocean.

❁ *The river of life carries everything away but the determined rocks don't budge.*

While the weak-minded hay floats away on the waters of possibility, the strong-willed rocks choose to stay grounded in reality.

Hours passed by with him just helplessly floating around in the ocean, till Lohajanga drifted off to sleep again. When he got up next there were two large pairs of eyes staring at him in great anger. He woke up with a start to find the elephant parked on the shores of an island and two huge warriors with horned helmets and massive spikes staring at him angrily with bloodshot eyes. They picked him up as if he was a little boy and carried him into the city. As they were carrying him into the city people stared at him in amazement as if he was from another planet.

On noticing the size of the people and the buildings around him, he realised that he had indeed come to a totally different world. Everything and everyone here was massive in size. Even the animals were gigantic. The two demons dragged him into the court of their king and threw him to the ground. They informed the king that after a really long time someone had dared to cross the ocean and come to their golden island. They warned the king that the last time also initially just one monkey had arrived. But it became a complete military invasion of millions of monkeys led by Lord Rama. They warned the king not to trust this man, however innocent he may seem. The fact that this man had managed to find a way to the island in spite of the bridge to Lanka being destroyed, only meant that he was very clever and completely untrustworthy. This definitely hinted at a possible siege of Lanka again.

Past bad experiences leave a permanent scar on your present conclusions.

King Vibhishan smiled at their over-protectiveness. He asked the traveller for an explanation. Lohajanga understood the context of the discussion and also realised where he had reached. He began to speak very sweetly to the king. He said, 'My dear king, let me first tell you how fortunate I feel to be in the presence of such a great king and an exalted devotee. I have been an ardent devotee of Lord Vishnu all my life and I performed unlimited austerities to please my lord. One day as I was in my prayers, I heard the voice of the lord urging me to go to Vibhishan. The lord reiterated multiple times that his devotee Vibhishan would surely offer me great wealth with which I can happily live out the rest of my life. I then prayed to the lord to somehow arrange for me to reach your island. After offering that prayer I slept and when I woke up, I found myself in your island. I have no idea how I reached so far from my hometown. This is all I know, my dear king, and this is the truth. It is up to you to believe me or not.'

The witty flourish where fools perish.

King Vibhishan liked the innocence projected by Lohajanga and decided to help him. He gave him many precious diamonds and the four symbols: shankha, chakra, gadha and padma of Lord Vishnu wrought in solid Lankan gold. In addition to these valuables, Vibhishan also gave him a huge kite, which could carry him back to his hometown. Mounting that massive bird, Lohajanga flew back to his hometown and landed on the outskirts of the city. He hid his wealth in a secret place and walked into the city in disguise. He sold one of the diamonds and did some shopping with the proceeds. He then sat under a tree and patiently waited for nightfall before taking action.

❁ *A win is born from a wit.*

In the middle of the night, the windows began to rattle and swing around noisily. The disturbance woke Rupinika up. Suddenly she heard the flapping of wings. It wasn't just from a regular bird; it was as if something huge was flapping its wings. As she sat up in puzzled trepidation a flash of light flooded her room. She winced and shielded her eyes from the blinding light that came in from the window. After a few seconds, when the intensity of the light reduced, she dropped her hands but what she saw made her scream. Suddenly, an arm came around her waist and a hand cupped her mouth, muffling her shriek.

She couldn't believe what she was seeing. It was her Lohajanga! But what had happened to him? He was dressed like Lord Vishnu. In fact he had the four symbols of Lord Vishnu. Once she had settled down, he removed the hand that covered her mouth and told her the whole story. She couldn't believe so much had happened in the last few days. But she was ecstatic that he had returned safely. Lohajanga explained the plan that he had in mind to her. She happily agreed to be a part of anything that he wanted. They spent hours together, exchanging loving words and heartfelt embraces. Just before dawn, Lohajanga got onto his bird carrier and flew away. Now it was Rupinika's turn to take the drama to the next level.

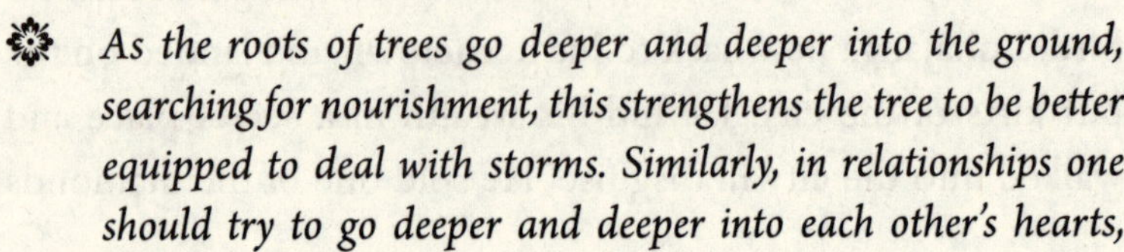

❁ *As the roots of trees go deeper and deeper into the ground, searching for nourishment, this strengthens the tree to be better equipped to deal with storms. Similarly, in relationships one should try to go deeper and deeper into each other's hearts,*

searching for nourishment. This strengthens the bond, enabling partners to face any storm.

The next morning Rupinika did not get out of her room. After calling her incessantly and waiting for several hours, Makaradarshtra pushed open the door to her room. She was surprised to see her daughter seated in a yogic posture with her back and erect eyes closed, focusing inwards. In spite of being called several times, she wasn't responding and seemed to be lost in another world. After several minutes, Rupinika opened her eyes. She had a subtle smile on her face and a look of deep satisfaction. Her mother was surprised at this transformation in her daughter. She asked if everything was all right and inquired about this sudden change in her.

✿ *Every change is not a transformation but every transformation is definitely a change.*

Rupinika explained that she was the chosen one on earth of Lord Vishnu. She told her about a dream she had last night where a divine voice told her that she would become the wife of Lord Vishnu and that the lord would be visiting her at night. In great excitement she explained how Lord Vishnu had appeared to her in the middle of the night seated on His bird carrier and had accepted her hand in marriage. Makaradarshtra was totally perplexed and did not know whether to believe her or not. Her daughter seemed so serious about the whole thing. In fact, the had started behaving like a goddess. Such a huge transformation in her daughter made her thoughtful. She decided not to question her but rather wait for the night to confirm it on her own.

Makaradarshtra kept vigil all night, stationing herself at a place from which she could easily keep watch on the window to her daughter's room. And lo and behold! At the stroke of midnight, a huge bird flew in, parking itself adjacent to the window. Mounted on the bird was undoubtedly Lord Vishnu, holding the four symbols made of shimmering gold in four hands. Bedecked gorgeously with opulent jewellery and sporting a golden crown, Lord Vishnu stepped into the room through the window. As soon as Lord Vishnu stepped in, the bird flew away. As soon as He stepped in, the room became effulgent, radiating light the likes of which she had never seen. For several hours, Lord Vishnu remained inside and then just before dawn he left. Makaradarshtra was thrilled. She was so happy that her daughter had indeed become a goddess.

She waited impatiently for a few more hours then rushed into her daughter's room to find her once again seated in a meditative pose. Makaradarshtra was going mad with happiness. She tried to be patient with her daughter and not express her desire immediately. But of course she couldn't hold it in for too long and it burst out. She begged her daughter to ask Lord Vishnu to take her to heaven while she was alive. Her daughter agreed to ask him on her behalf.

❁ *Just as the ground cannot hold a seed inside for too long and soon bursts out as a plant, similarly the heart cannot hold desires for too long, it soon bursts out.*

The next day her daughter told her that Lord Vishnu considered her very sinful and that she was not eligible to enter the heavens. But if she did something that he prescribed, it would absolve her of all sin and gain her entry there. She had to be ready the next day, early in the morning, before dawn. Since it was the twelfth day or Dwadashi, the gates to heaven opened for a short duration at sunrise. That was the time when the goblins of Lord Shiva entered heaven. Lord Vishnu had promised that He could try to push her mother in along with Lord Shiva's goblins. But the only prerequisite was that her mother should look like a goblin of Lord Shiva. Lord Vishnu described what a goblin of Lord Shiva would look like.

Dressed as per the instructions of Lord Vishnu, Makaradarshtra stood waiting. Lord Vishnu spent some time with Rupinika and then summoned her mother. Taking her along with Him on His bird carrier, He dropped her on top of the temple spire, telling her that this was the collection point for the goblins of Lord Shiva. She would be picked up at the right time and taken to the heavens. Her joy knew no bounds knowing that only in a short while from now, she would be in the heavens experiencing its divine pleasures.

After dropping her, Lohajanga changed to his regular appearance and entered the city. He began to spread a rumour that Goddess Mara would fall from the temple dome that morning and her fall would mean the destruction of the whole world. The rumour, along with people spotting Makaradarshtra on top of the temple, created the desired effect and soon the whole city had gathered by the temple. By now Makaradarshtra realised that she had been fooled and fear took hold of her. When that boy recognised her and everyone began to laugh at her plight, Makaradarshtra's pride was quelled. After she was brought down by the king, no one ever saw her again. She remained confined within her home and did not trouble anyone else ever again.

 *Those who trouble others are actually borrowing trouble for themselves.*

When the king heard the whole story from Lohajanga, he was very pleased at his courage and his loyalty to his beloved. He took the prince to task at once for misusing his powers. As far as Makaradarshtra was concerned, she had already been punished enough. She had the rest of her life to repent for all the wrongs that she had done.

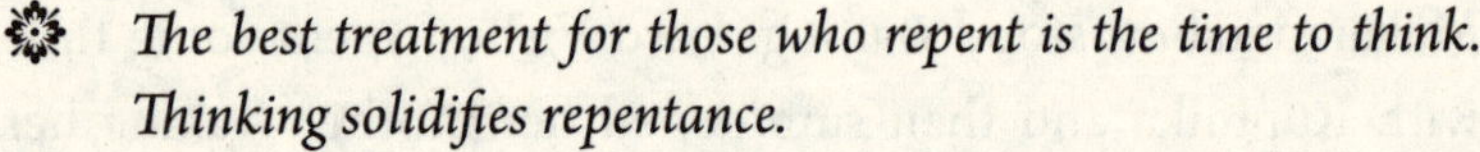

The best treatment for those who repent is the time to think. Thinking solidifies repentance.

Lohajanga and Rupinika got married and remained happy and loyal to each other forever. The bird returned to Vibhishan and the four symbols of Lord Vishnu were offered by the king to the Vishnu temple to be placed in the hands of Lord Vishnu to whom they rightfully belonged.

As Vasavadatta heard the story of the determination of Lohajanga to make Rupinika his life partner, she became determined to have Udayana as her life partner. As Vasantaka spoke about how the loving moments the couple spent together had strengthened their relationship, enabling them to face every challenge together, she fondly remembered all the loving moments she had spent with Udayana. As Vasantaka narrated trouble after trouble, problem after problem, difficulty after difficulty, Vasavadatta readied herself to face any difficulty to make Udayana her husband. She was even ready to defy her father to be with Udayana. The twist in that story led to a twist in this story. At the end of the storytelling session, Udayana and Vasavadatta were in each other's arms. Having accomplished his goal, Vasantaka quietly walked out.

❁ *When you need inspiration look for a good story. Stories have the power to help you create your own story.*

King Chandamsena was totally unaware of the deep love that had awakened between the two youngsters. While Vasantaka and Yaugandharayana kept the king distracted with their jests, Udayana and Vasavadatta were ensconced in their musical love. A few days later, as planned, Vasavadatta managed to get her elephant Bhadravati stationed outside city limits. Udayana and Vasavadatta, accompanied by Vasantaka and Yaugandharayana, left the palace through a secret underground tunnel. Kanchanamala, who was Vasavadatta's maidservant, also tagged along at the last minute. All night, the retinue travelled through the dense forest path. Bhadravati moved non-stop over hills, valleys, thick forests and deep rivers. Not for one moment did the loyal elephant stop to rest. When they managed to cross the dense Vindhya Mountains, which had been the toughest part of the journey, the elephant fell down dead. As they were lamenting the loss of their dear saviour, a celestial voice was heard. 'O King! Please know that I am actually a Vidyadhara woman named Mayavati and had been cursed to be in the body of an elephant for many years. The curse had also prophesied that once I helped you in your mission, I would regain my celestial form. You should also know that Vasavadatta is no ordinary woman. She is a goddess and has been born as a woman only to be united with you.'

❁ *Some people's presence is felt even in their absence while others' absence is felt even in their presence.*

Soon the retinue reached their kingdom, where Udayana married Vasavadatta amidst great pomp and festivity. King Chandamsena was shocked and angry on getting reports of his daughter eloping with his enemy Udayana. Though he did want Udayana as his son-in-law, he had not wanted it to come about in his way. For many months Chandamsena did not accept the marriage. But when he got the news that Vasavadatta had given birth to a beautiful boy named Naravahanadatta, the grandfather's heart melted.

❁ *The relationships that we want to work on our terms are those relationships that never work.*

King Udayana led a blissful life with his wife and son Naravahanadatta, who was personally blessed by Narada Muni. Just like his father, Udayana also quit his responsibilities as a king at the right time and handed over the reins to his able son and proceeded towards the Himalayas with his lifelong companion Vasavadatta. Every king in this dynasty lived like a hero and left like a saint!

❁ *An ideal life is to live like a hero and leave like a saint.*

GOOD TIMES HELP TIDE OVER BAD TIMES

Spending time together is more important than spending a life together. Time is the world's most expensive currency. When you invest time on something or someone, it means that you are investing your most expensive currency in that person. Probably the best way to understand your priorities is to monitor the way you spend the currency of time.

This is a story of two couples who invested time in each other. Though it may seem to be a small detail in the two intertwined stories, it is really the essence of the two stories. Udayana and Vasavadatta as well as Lohajanga and Rupinika built their relationships based on quality time spent in each other's company. This not only builds a relationship but is also an investment that saves it from dwindling. Whatever we invest time in, grows. If we invest time in business, it grows. If we invest time in knowledge, it grows. If we invest time in negativity, it grows. If we invest time in love, it grows. Time is one venture that always brings you returns. The two couples invested time in each other and it brought them returns by bringing them closer.

Spending time together is about building a database of good memories. Time spent together is saved as memories. A life spent together is saved as dates. Good memories act as the threads that weave two independent lives together. All the decisions of investments we make are based on our feelings. We invest in those things that we like. One may say that decisions are made based on logic and intelligence. Yes that may be enough to weigh the pros and cons, but the final call is always motivated by feelings. Therefore building a bank of good memories is crucial for relationships to be sustained. We are more likely to invest time in a relationship where there is a bank of good memories which will propel us to invest more time in it. The investment of time and the building of memories thus become cyclic.

Every meeting between Lohajanga and Rupinika built wonderful memories. Every meeting between Udayana and Vasavadatta also built wonderful memories. Every memory inspired them to invest more time in each other in spite of the odd circumstances they found themselves in. All the time they spent together was invested in creating memorable moments.

It's not only about the quantity of time but about the quality of time spent together that really matters. It is better to experience one moment of full attention than a million moments of half-attention. Often people who stay together but spend only 'quantity time' with each other end up feeling lonely. Perhaps the greatest need of a human heart is the need to be understood. Anyone who spends quality time trying to understand the other person wins their heart.

Very often people think that spending time is about talking. In reality, the most important part of a healthy interaction is about listening. Listening is different from hearing. Most people hear the words being spoken but those who value healthy relationships listen to the feelings behind the words. Most people either don't listen or pretend to listen or listen selectively or self-centredly. But those who value relationships listen empathetically, with a desire to understand. Only when you meet someone who understands you do you realise that you are not self-sufficient.

Lohajanga put his heart into listening to Rupinika, desiring only to understand what she was going through. While the whole world looked upon her with disdain, he was the only person who appreciated her without judging her for her connection with her mother and the house of ill-repute in which she lived. For the first time Rupinika found someone who was trying his best to understand her without allowing any bias or preconceived notion to come in between. She felt so connected that she dedicated her life to him.

Vasavadatta's father wanted her to marry Udayana but did not understand his need for respect. Vasavadatta simply spent time respecting him for who he was and not pushing him to do something he wasn't comfortable with. What the father couldn't achieve by force, the daughter achieved by showing respect. In this way Udayana finally found someone who genuinely empathised with him.

When people feel understood, they want to understand in return. Alignment is important for relationships to last. Alignment is about sitting in the same vehicle, facing the same direction and moving towards the same destination. Many a time it happens that people who live together are found to be sitting in different vehicles, facing different directions and moving towards different destinations. And they don't understand why their relationship failed. To align with one another, two people need to have deep, meaningful, soul-searching conversations. These conversations are about revealing one's thoughts, feelings and fears to one another without inhibitions and with utter honesty. After all sharing is caring and caring is about understanding.

When one feels understood, one develops self-worth. Most often people don't realise that self-worth is connected with being understood. People who have low self-esteem are the ones who have never experienced being understood in their lives. When your self-worth is enhanced, you can conquer the world. You also naturally invest more time in the relationship that enhances your self-worth, thereby strengthening it further.

Lohajanga invested time in understanding Rupinika. Therefore she invested time in understanding him. Before he met her, he was a simple and non-enterprising man. But with the boost in self-worth he experienced in her company, Lohajanga turned into a hero. He went on to accept challenges the magnitude of which would put any hero to shame. Just because he felt understood, he grew in his own eyes.

Every person experiences good and bad times in life. Everyone has a million ways of enjoying the good times. But when it comes to experiencing the bad times, there is only one way that people know: suffering them painfully. The good memories made with people you love become a source of solace you dip into to handle the bad times with dignity and grace. Relationships where sufficient investments have been made during good times actually become stronger during bad times. Good times spent together help during the inevitable bad times together.

Lohajanga and Rupinika dealt with the storm that came into their life with such intelligence and mutual coordination that it brought them the greatest stability in their lives. Udayana and Vasavadatta spent such good times together that their relationship was only enhanced during the bad times. Both couples experienced joy and sorrow. If the good times enhanced their bond, then the bad times only strengthened it further.

Get away from the toxicity of loneliness; try the nectar of investing time in someone. It may not only help you feel less lonely but may act as a catalyst for self-growth. Growth in a relationship brings about growth in an individual.

Chapter 5

THE WOMAN WHO CHOSE

'Exactly one year from now, he will die!'

The proclamation of a celestial of the stature of Narada Muni shattered the heart of the father. His daughter was determined to marry a man who was destined to die soon. The concerned father was determined to prevent this tragedy. After all Savitri was his only child and had been born as a result of him undertaking eighteen years of rigorous austerities and sacrifices aimed at pleasing Goddess Savitri. After the birth of the gorgeous baby girl, the proud father, King Ashwapati, gratefully named her Savitri. Never did he imagine that his precious daughter would make such a terrible choice.

Narada Muni emphasised upon his point. 'Satyavan has the best qualities a man can have and more. He is as energetic as the sun itself and is as wise as Brihaspati, the teacher of the devatas. He is as heroic as Indra and simultaneously as forgiving as the earth. He is as charitable as Rantideva and as devoted to truthfulness as Shibi. He is as magnanimous as Yayati and as charming as the moon. His beauty puts the twin Ashwini Kumaras to shame. Moreover he is highly self-controlled, humble, faithful, free from malice and very patient. In essence there could be no better man in this universe than Satyavan. But one defect eclipses all these superlative qualities and makes him unfit for marriage. He is destined to die exactly a year from now.'

✿ *Just as one ant in the ear of a huge elephant throws it off completely, sometimes a tiny defect in a human being, amongst oodles of good qualities, messes up his life completely.*

Narada Muni's serious tone made Ashwapati tremble. Turning to his daughter he said, 'My dear girl, choose someone else as your husband. You made your choice while you were ignorant of the sword hanging on his head. This fact surpasses all his merits.'

'My dear father, you know well that everyone dies just once. But you should also know that one gives one's heart also just once. Having given my heart to Satyavan, I cannot think of giving myself to anyone else. Whether one has a long or short life is never in one's hands. But whether one has good or bad qualities is definitely in one's hands. As far as destiny is concerned, it is like a flowing river. Just as a flowing river changes its course, destiny too is flexible enough in its course. Our future destiny is organically created by our present actions. If everything was frozen, what is the meaning of any choice we make? If everything was pre-destined then what is the role of human ambition? The length of life is never as important as its depth. The quantitative time spent in a relationship is never as important as the qualitative time spent relishing it. As far as death itself is concerned, at least we know for sure that Satyavan will live for a year but do we know for how long we will live? Can we be sure that we will live even another day? The mind that doesn't settle on one thing can never settle on anything. Having given my heart to Satyavan, I cannot think of any other person to lead my life with.' Savitri spoke with such conviction and logic that everyone present was stupefied. The beauty of her form was complemented elegantly by the beauty of her astute intelligence.

❁ *Destiny is as flexible as soft clay and not rigid like a hard stone that cannot be reshaped.*

One moment of attentive love is better than a million moments of struggling to love.

Narada Muni smiled in delight. He hadn't come across anyone with such clear thinking thus far. Impressed with Savitri's conviction, he declared, 'O King, indeed Savitri has chosen well. There is none like Satyavan in merit and there is none like Savitri in determination. Wherever we find great virtue followed by great determination, there is always victory and prosperity.'

The words of the great sage brought joy to King Ashwapati who immediately began to make arrangements for the royal wedding. On reaching the hermitage of King Dyumatsena which was in the middle of a forest, King Ashwapati walked in with a group of brahmanas, carrying auspicious gifts for the former king. It was a sad sight to behold. The once-powerful monarch had been reduced to a pitiable condition. At one point the kingdom of Shalya had been a formidable empire with flourishing resources and opportunities. Fate struck one day when the king was declared to be going blind. As his eyesight waned, so did his followers. In due course King Dyumatsena faced a humiliating defeat at the hands of his neighbouring king. Somehow saving his own life and that of his family, the blind king fled in a desperate attempt to salvage what was left. Of course back then Satyavan, his son, was an infant. Deprived of his kingdom and his sight, the king chose to go on an internal journey. Austerities and penances became the norm in his life and his only associates were the great sages of the forest. That was the atmosphere in which Satyavan was raised. In the midst of the dreary forest he stood out like a rare gem.

❁ *It is often seen that when your ability to contribute to people decreases, people's abilities to love you decrease as well.*

When King Ashwapati set his eyes on Satyavan, he was highly impressed. His daughter had definitely made a wise choice. In all fourteen worlds, there couldn't be a better match for Savitri. His handsome mien and his charming personality had pleased the king. But more than the externals, what really made him stand apart were his genuine kindness and his loving nature. That really touched the hearts of all the visitors. The sages in the forest told the king that the boy was named Satyavan because he had been born to two of the most truthful humans on earth at that time. Satyavan was true to his name. He was the epitome of integrity and truthfulness.

❁ *In the beginning of life your name defines you; by the end of life you should define your name.*

After the welcoming ceremony was completed, the blind king Dyumatsena asked Ashwapati the reason for his undertaking the journey to visit his dilapidated hermitage. Without mincing words, King Ashwapati explained that his daughter, the beautiful Savitri, had fallen in love with Satyavan and had decided to take no one but him as her husband. King Ashwapati expressed his appreciation for Satyavan and requested the blind king for his opinion about the alliance. With tears trickling down his eyes, Dyumatsena held Ashwapati's hand.

'Your daughter is a delicate angel. Having been brought up in royal comfort, how will she be able to adjust to the rigour of forest life?' the blind king asked with genuine concern.

'Nothing in this world is permanent. Neither pleasure nor pain. Neither happiness nor misery. Both my daughter and I have internalised this philosophy. We wholeheartedly accept the non-permanence of life as the ultimate reality and the permanence of relationships as the ultimate harbinger of satisfaction in life,' Ashwapati expressed with great clarity. 'Please accept my daughter as your daughter-in-law. I have come with great expectations from you. I consider you an old friend and an equal in every way; I am requesting you to accept this alliance between Satyavan and Savitri.'

✿ *Only when one accepts the non-permanence of life as the ultimate reality and the permanence of relationships as the ultimate harbinger of satisfaction in life, is one duly admitted to the school of life.*

The old blind king staggered up. Taking hold of Ashwapati's shoulder he said, 'O Ashwapati, when I used to be a king ages ago, I had very much desired an alliance with you, knowing you to be an embodiment of goodness. But once I lost my kingdom, I lost the courage to even think of approaching you. Your coming here is a fortuitous opportunity for me to re-live my dream.'

The moment the kings agreed, Satyavan and Savitri looked at each other and smiled. This wasn't their first meeting. They had met before. In fact, not only once but several times in a short span. The very moment they had seen each other, something had clicked. Something deep inside their hearts.

Savitri's father had been on the lookout for a suitable groom for her. Every match that he brought to her was rejected outright by her. Even those few select grooms that Savitri chose to meet didn't last beyond a few sentences. Savitri's philosophy and thought process was way beyond the ordinary. Her determination and grit were incomprehensible to regular humans. Her ideas and thoughts gave them an inferiority complex and they would find it highly uncomfortable to take part in any sort of discussion with her. When her father saw that this was not going to be easy at all, he decided to try something different. He told her that since nothing seemed to be working out from his side, he was setting her free to travel around and find her own match.

 *For those who have grit, 'NO' appears to be 'ON'.*

Grit is a worm inside the human body that continuously forces one to never accept no for an answer.

As instructed by her father, Savitri wandered across the world looking for her life partner. Most qualified princes and kings that she came across, she rejected at first sight. There was no question of a closer interaction when she felt repulsed on sight. It was not that they were ugly or deformed. They were some of the most handsome and charismatic men in the world. But she was in search of something else. Something in someone that would touch her heart like no other. That was when she encountered Satyavan in the middle of the forest. The moment she set her eyes on him, she felt drawn like an iron filing is drawn towards a magnet. The attraction was spontaneous and irresistible. Suddenly she found herself standing in front of this handsome man. She had no idea who he was. She had no idea why she was attracted to him. All she knew was that this was the first time in her life that she had been drawn to someone so intensely.

 *When physical attraction becomes a mental connection, then relationships become loveships.*

The first words that escaped Satyavan's mouth made her gasp. All he said were some pleasantries, but there was magic in his voice. She desperately waited for the next word so she could savour it like nectar. It took her a few minutes to gather herself and have a meaningful conversation with him. She introduced herself as a lost princess who needed help. Satyavan readily offered to help her in his chivalrous way. In fact he arranged for accommodation for her in the house of one of the hermits dwelling in the forest. Ensuring that she would be cared for by the ladies of the hermitage, Satyavan left. Savitri smiled and kept smiling through the whole night.

When smiles take over your nights instead of sleep, that's when you know that someone has taken over your life.

The next morning when he saw her standing at the exact same place with the exact same smile, he couldn't help but smile himself. That very moment their bond came into being. As Satyavan expertly helped Savitri traverse the path through the forest, he shared the wisdom of the forest with her. He showed her numerous small details about the trees, creepers, insects, birds and animals that an untrained eye would completely miss. In those few hours she spent with Satyavan, she felt as if she had grown in every way. By the time they reached the outer limits of the forest, from where there was a clear path to her kingdom, Savitri was completely convinced that her search for an ideal partner was complete. She did not have to look any further.

 *The best people to spend time with are those who expedite your personal growth.*

And here they were, looking at each other once again. The same smile gleamed on both their faces. The only difference was that this time behind Savitri's smile was a hidden sadness. The words of Sage Narada rang in her ears constantly. She kept hearing his warnings and his advice to her to stay away from this relationship that could only be short-lived. Though she had won her father over with lofty words, she knew in her heart of hearts that defying destiny was next to impossible. She shuddered to think that they had just one year to experience all the love they had in their hearts and souls. What would follow was a lifetime of lonely misery. But she also knew that without being united with Satyavan her life would be equally miserable. This is why she had taken the tough decision of choosing one year of union with the person she loved so dearly. And then would arrive that tryst with destiny.

❁ *Smiles are often the deepest cries of the heart.*

Always fix your appointment with your destiny in the skies of hope and not on the grounds of fear.

Sweeping her sadness aside, Savitri focussed on the present. They united with their parents' and close well-wishers' blessings. Savitri and her father Ashwapati chose to keep Sage Narada's prophecy a secret. Not wanting to disturb the peaceful and happy family atmosphere with this disturbing news, they decided to focus on the happiness that the coming one year promised them.

❁ *In enjoying the good that hasn't happened and suffering the bad that hasn't happened, people forget to experience the life that's happening.*

As soon as her parents left for their kingdom, Savitri shed all her ornaments and silken clothing and donned the coarse wear made of tree bark and deer skin that was common in the hermitage. Through her good qualities, amiable behaviour, attitude of service, self-control, sweet demeanour and carefully chosen, sensitive words, Savitri won the heart of her father-in-law and mother-in-law. Satyavan was highly impressed with her ability to touch people's hearts so deeply. Anyone who spent even a few moments with her would develop a deep affection for her.

Savitri was most happy in Satyavan's loving company. Everything that Satyavan did and said made her fall deeper in love with him. Satyavan also cherished her beautiful company. Never had he seen anyone with more compassion than her. It extended not only to humans but even to tender creepers. The newly married couple spent hours together every day, building a deep connection with each other. Appreciation and sweet words flowed freely between them making their hearts overflow with joy. They also spent a substantial amount of time in soul-searching conversations with the great sages of the forest and learnt deep meditation techniques from them. However, no matter what she did, that one single disturbing thought would always niggle at the back of her mind. It was like a smudged backdrop on which nothing, no matter how good, would be visible.

 *There is a mouth to ear channel that helps to fill the love tank in the heart. When words of appreciation, encouragement and love flow profusely from one's mouth to another's ear, it fills the love tank in their hearts.*

Soul-searching conversations are the food on which the human soul thrives in the deserts of loneliness and directionlessness.

Time is relative in nature. When one experiences good times, it rushes past like the raging wind. But when one experiences bad times, it stagnates like the stink of a garbage can. The good times of Satyavan and Savitri's life came to a close with the completion of the one-year period that Narada Muni had indicated. Savitri was desperately aware of the ticking of time, while Satyavan was blissfully unaware of it.

❁ *Good times pass quickly and pain passes slowly. Life keeps changing the pace of time.*

Four days prior to the day Narada Muni had earmarked, Savitri disclosed the disturbing news to Satyavan's parents. The news shattered them. When they saw their son tending to his duties, totally unaware of the impending calamity, they felt wretched. Not wanting to show him their distress, they acted normally around him. But every time they spoke to him or heard him speak, their hearts felt like they were about to be ripped open, breaking the dam of self-restraint they had imposed upon themselves. Their admiration for Savitri only increased. She had managed to hold on to this news for nearly a year, while they were struggling to contain themselves for even a day. At the end of the day Savitri declared to them and to her husband Satyavan that for the next three days she would be undertaking a fast known as Triratra. She would be fasting continuously for the next three days and nights, completely abstaining from food or drink. At the end of the third night and the beginning of the fourth morning she would break her fast. The third night of her fast would be the night of her tryst with destiny.

❁ *Holding disturbing news in the mind is holding burning coal in the hand. Till you drop it there is no peace.*

Though Satyavan kept dissuading her, telling her that such extreme austerity was unnecessary, she wouldn't budge. Satyavan's parents remained mum, unable to say anything. His parents knew the reason for the fast but couldn't share it with their son. Their once happy world was crumbling right in front of their eyes and they couldn't do anything. For once, Dyumatsena was grateful that he was blind. He only wished he had been blind to the realities of life as well. At this point he felt that there was nothing compared to the pain of knowledge and there was nothing compared to the bliss of ignorance. They were aware but miserable while Satyavan was ignorant but blissful.

 *The more blissful the ignorance, the more painful the reality of life.*

Savitri began her intense austerities. Sitting on the mud floor with an erect back and closed eyes for hours together, she seemed to resemble a block of wood. Unwavering and immobile, Savitri continued her fervent vow. At the end of the first day, Dyumatsena tried to talk her out of it. With complete confidence she explained to him that she was determined not to allow destiny to take Satyavan away from her. Anyone who has collided with destiny has to be more determined than destiny itself. These three days were nothing but a test of her determination to keep Satyavan in her life forever. Dyumatsena had tears in his eyes at Savitri's determination. Never in his life had he seen anyone so determined to make a relationship last for life. While most people give up on a relationship when things don't work out or when their natures don't match, here was a person determined to challenge nature itself to make the relationship last for a lifetime.

 *Do not underestimate the role of determination in a relationship. Ordinary relationships transform into extraordinary bonds when ordinary people show extraordinary determination.*

When the three-day period ended, Savitri had become fairly emaciated. Her in-laws requested her to break her fast by eating something. Savitri was hardly bothered about food or water. She realised that this was the most crucial point in her husband's life. She had to be with him. Anything could happen, anytime. As she turned around looking for Satyavan, she spotted him at a far distance taking a turn around the corner of the forest path. He was carrying a hatchet in his hand. Holding it over his shoulders, he was walking into the forest to fetch some firewood. Savitri realised that this was the moment she had dreaded all year long. Satyavan was walking into the forest alone. She felt strongly that she had to be with him. Savitri got up abruptly. Her frail legs wobbled as she stood on them. She had been seated in one place for three consecutive days and her legs had gone numb. As she stood up, trying to rush out of the hermitage, she fell over as she lost her balance and almost hit her head on the doorway. Holding on to whatever she could, Savitri steadied herself and rushed in the direction Satyavan was headed. Yelling his name, urging him to stop, she rushed towards her partner like a madwoman.

Satyavan heard his wife's shrill cries and slowed down. He waited for her to catch up with him, wondering what had upset her so much. He would set out to fetch firewood every day at this time, and his wife had never accompanied him on this chore. Something didn't seem right. He still hadn't understood the reason for her excruciatingly painful vow of fasting, and now this episode of madly running after him. There was something in her mind that was disturbing her. Understanding that somebody who was disturbed didn't need advice as much as they needed hope, Satyavan decided to give her hope through his words.

❁ *A disturbed person is looking for hope, not advice.*

Holding her hand tightly, he began to walk deeper into the woods. He kept talking about all the beautiful things that they could see around them. He stopped every now and then, pointing out a bird or a flower and explaining their uniqueness. He tried to lighten her mood. However, Savitri couldn't bear laughing or even smiling. She kept staring at her husband's happy face. She kept watching for any sign of fatigue or disturbance in his body language. According to her calculations, this was the fatal moment. But he seemed perfectly all right. Satyavan began to gather fruits and handing them over to Savitri. After a short while, he stopped by a tree which he found suitable for firewood. Gripping his hatchet tightly, he began to strike with great force at its trunk. As the splinters of wood went flying, Savitri began to think, could the celestials be wrong in their calculations and predictions? Wasn't this the moment...

❁ *The only thing predictable about the future is that it's unpredictable.*

Just then Satyavan's hand began to loosen its grip on the hatchet. A sudden tremor arose in his hands. He turned towards Savitri with wide open eyes. There was fear in them. Beads of perspiration began to trickle down his forehead. Savitri gripped his hand tightly. His knees began to quiver. He wasn't able to stand on his feet anymore. Stooping, he held onto the ground. He squatted, supporting himself against a tree. Holding his head in one hand and clutching Savitri's hand in the other, he began to look around fearfully. His hatchet had fallen somewhere. His upper garment was drenched in sweat. Savitri placed his head on her lap and began to wipe the sweat dripping down his forehead with the edge of her sari. Though she was trembling in fear, since she understood that the end had come, she decided that she would do her best to be strong.

'O this pain is unbearable. It feels as if my head is being pierced by thousands of sharp arrows. Every limb in my body is aching fiercely. I don't know what's happening to me. A sudden fear has gripped my heart. A type of fear that I have never known. Savitri, stay next to me and hold ...' Satyavan spoke to his wife while staring into the distance, as if he was seeing something in the dark woods. Then, mid-sentence, Satyavan passed out.

As Savitri began to attempt to bring Satyavan back to consciousness, she felt a movement. She froze. The dark shadow of a huge figure loomed over them. As it came closer, it began to grow till they were completely enveloped by the dark blanket of the shadow. Squinting her eyes Savitri strained to see who it was. Attired in red garments and sporting a large golden crown, a humungous personality with a reddish gold complexion and blood red eyes stood next to Satyavan's unconscious body, holding a noose in one hand and a mace in the other. His facial expression was as grave as death.

Gently placing her husband's head on the ground, Savitri stood up with joined palms and a respectful demeanour. Though her body was trembling, her voice was stable. 'From your superhuman look, I can recognise that you are a god. O divine personality, please reveal to me who you are!'

'O pure-hearted Savitri, your ability to see me is a result of your purity and devotion. Know me to be Yama, the god of death. Your husband's time is up and I have come to transport him to his next destination.' With a thunderous voice that boomed through the silent forest, Yama spelled out his intentions clearly.

Savitri realised that this was the moment she had been preparing for during the past one year. Keeping herself as cool and composed as possible externally, though internally completely shaken, Savitri spoke to Yama. 'O invincible god of death, I have heard that your able assistants do the job of taking away departed souls to the abode of death. How is it that you have chosen to come yourself in the case of my husband?'

❁ *Life is a preparation for just one moment of action. That defining moment in everyone's life represents everything one has learnt, experienced, followed and believed in.*

'Yes, that is the general norm. But I felt that none of my men were qualified enough to bring in a person of the calibre of Satyavan. His virtues are as vast as the ocean and my men are capable of handling only ordinary people. Now allow me to carry out my duties, O saintly lady.'

Yama quickly threw his noose around Satyavan's limp body. The mystical rope disappeared into his body. With a jerk Yama pulled it out. Fastened to the noose was the tiny soul of Satyavan. The lifeless body of her husband was lying exactly where she had left him, but the soul of Satyavan, which was the size of a human thumb, had been freed from his body and was being pulled by Yama towards his own abode in a southerly direction. Savitri realised that her husband did not reside in that lifeless body anymore and began to follow Satyavan's soul, which was being taken away by Yama.

Seeing her follow him, Yama stopped and turned to face her. 'Please go back, Savitri. Your duties towards your husband are completed. Now you must ensure that the cremation of his body is completed. This is the farthest you are allowed to come. Mortals from earth are not allowed to traverse beyond this limit.'

Love that is temporary cannot belong to the soul that is permanent.

Human commitments that last are always done at the level of the soul.

'My duty is to accompany my husband wherever he goes. Whether he goes of his own accord or is being carried away by force, that doesn't matter. And I know very well that due to my devotion and determination, no force will be able to prevent me from accompanying my husband. Wise men say that two people who walk seven paces together become friends. If we keep that definition in mind, then we have both walked ten paces together. Aren't we friends then? Let me offer a small piece of wisdom to my newly found friend…' Savitri kept talking just to keep Yama's attention. She knew that once he left the earthly realms and ascended to the heavenly abodes, she wouldn't be able to do much. Yama smiled at her comment. Never had anyone spoken to him like that. It amused him. Looking at her he stopped and smiled, indicating that he was ready to hear the advice that she was so eager to give.

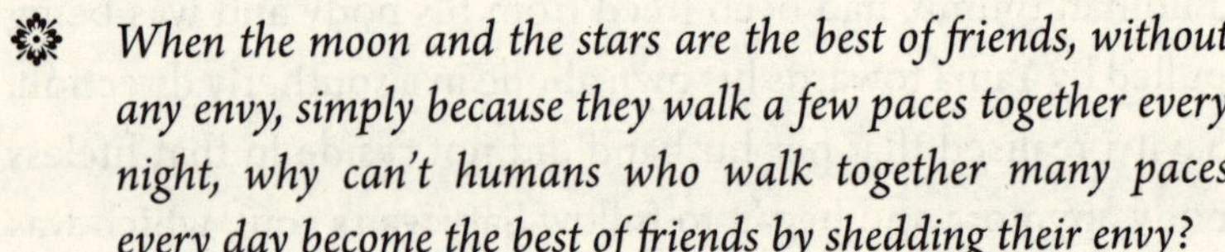

When the moon and the stars are the best of friends, without any envy, simply because they walk a few paces together every night, why can't humans who walk together many paces every day become the best of friends by shedding their envy?

'Anyone who keeps the company of holy people never faces any grief in their life. By the power of their virtuous conduct holy people never face any sorrow in their life and that effect rubs off on anyone who is in their company. Such company is forever rewarding and ever beneficial. It is by the power of saintly people that the sun rises and it by their power that the earth is upheld. Such illustrious people help each other in the conduct of dharma. Rather than harbour animosity towards one another, great people help each other and thus act as co-protectors of the whole world.'

 *No one can grow by having wrong companions.*

No wonder people in the past would seek the company of holy people who would come together to achieve a common goal, forgetting their own petty concerns.

Yama was spellbound. 'Impressive! Great to hear such a revelation from you, Savitri. Every word you speak has such wisdom and yet such sweetness. You have touched my heart by your words. Let me offer you a boon. O pure lady, ask for any boon except the life of your husband. I will grant you anything you desire that is within my power.'

Savitri smiled and said, 'O great lord, if you do want to grant me a boon, I request you to restore my old father-in-law's eyesight. He has been living a life of abject poverty in the forest for so many decades. With his restored eyesight, let him rule the world like the sun.'

'Granted! The monarch will regain his eyes and rule his kingdom as before. Now go back and take care of your in-laws. Perform your duties to the dead and those that live.' Yama turned to leave.

'I want to share one more thought with you. You are the controller of all living beings. However, your control is not whimsical but based on established laws and regulations, which are in turn based on the principles of righteousness. If you ask me what the constitutional duty of the righteous is, I would say it is mercy and charity. There is no greater righteous act than benevolence and kindness towards everyone in creation. The righteous are ready to show such compassion not only towards those following the path of righteousness but also towards their enemies. In fact, the greats hold compassion in higher esteem than disciplining.' Savitri spoke with no fear in her eyes and with great confidence in her belief.

'Bravo! Bravo! This is simply nectar flowing from your lips. Your words as they flow into my ears are akin to water to a thirsty man. I am inspired to grant you another boon. Ask for anything except the life of your husband.' Yama was pretty impressed with Savitri's intelligence.

 *People are inspired by Lord Shiva because he carries the moon on his head and holds poison in his throat.*

People are inspired by those who have cool minds and who don't let poison come out of their mouths.

Inspired words come from inspired minds.

Savitri said, 'If you want to offer me a boon then let my father have many sons who would continue his legacy. I am his only child and don't even stay with him now. It would be beneficial if he had children who would assist him in handling the immense burden of ruling such a big empire.'

'Granted, Savitri, granted! Now please return and allow me to carry out my duty. Retrace your steps and return. You have come further than you are allowed. You must be tired after your fast and today's intensely disturbing episode.' Yama didn't mince words in instructing her to return.

Savitri smiled. 'Distances and troubles don't matter to me as long as I am beside my husband. Let me share with you one more thought that you might appreciate. You are the son of the sun god Vaivasvata. Just as the sun is impartial in bestowing its light and heat on everyone, similarly you judge all living entities impartially and fairly. People have more faith in such virtuous impartial souls than they have in themselves. Therefore everyone wants to cultivate friendships with such exalted beings. When confidence is bestowed upon such righteous souls, it leads to confidence in oneself. Great souls have the ability to pull out the virtuous person that is hidden deep within each individual.'

❁ *The goodness in a human feels like an alien in a strange planet and prefers to stay hidden.*

Great souls can spot the hidden goodness in every individual and also have the ability to create a familiar atmosphere where they can come and dance joyfully.

Yama was amazed at her intelligence. 'O great lady, never before have I heard such wisdom. I am very pleased with you. Ask me for one more boon. Anything except your husband's life.'

'If you want to offer me another boon, then let me have a hundred sons born of Satyavan from my womb, who will perpetuate our family and rule the world. I pray you grant me this boon,' Savitri earnestly pleaded with Yama.

'So be it! You will have a hundred sons who will become a source of unlimited pleasure for you. Now I request you to come no further. Return to your in-laws and live the rest of your life.' Yama turned around to resume his journey.

Savitri did not turn back even then. She continued speaking. She said, 'Pious people are extremely devoted to the practices that facilitate dharma. Such inclination to dharma destroys misery in this world. Such pious people live their lives sacrificing their own self-interest for the sake of others' welfare with absolutely no expectation whatsoever in return. Though they do not expect anything in return for their good deeds, such good deeds almost always become harbingers of auspiciousness in their lives. In fact, the very good deeds one does become the protectors of one's honour and interests.'

❁ *Good things are always found deep within the earth. They are tough to extract but once brought out, become the costliest things on earth.*

Similarly, goodness resides deep within the heart and is seldom exhibited, but once brought out it becomes the harbinger of not just joy but also goodness from all around.

Yama was thrilled. Every word she spoke simply amazed him to the core. He was so happy to hear her beautiful words, which held deep meaning and wisdom. He said, 'O divine lady, everything you say resonates so much in my heart that I am compelled to grant you one more boon. Choose such a boon, the type of which has never been chosen in the past.'

'My dear sir, the previous boon that you have granted me cannot be completed until my husband Satyavan becomes alive once again. If you want to grant me another boon, then may Satyavan be brought back to life. That is the only way this and your previous boon would be fulfilled. I do not want any opulence or pleasure without my husband by my side. You have promised me a boon of having a hundred sons through Satyavan and now you yourself are carrying him away. To prove your words to be true, the only way is to bring back my husband to life.' Savitri spoke with impeccable logic and fell silent.

❁ *Good logic shuts your mouth and opens your mind.*

Yama was confused. No one had ever managed to confuse him so much. Nor had anyone affected his emotions so much. The grip he had on the rope that held the noose around Satyavan's soul loosened automatically. He smiled to himself and let go completely. Satyavan's soul rushed back at lightning speed and disappeared as it went around the curve to where his body lay. Yama looked at Savitri and smiled.

❁ *Using their intelligence some people can dip into your mind and intensely affect your emotions.*

'O gentle lady, I have released your husband from my clutches. Take him back. He will now be free from all disease and live a long life. He will be renowned throughout the world for his greatness. But, most of all, he will be known for being your husband. He will be known as Savitri's Satyavan. And every other boon that you asked for will also be fulfilled. Go and live a life of joy and prosperity.' Yama disappeared the next instant.

A moan reached Savitri's ears and she ran as fast as her legs could carry her. Reaching the place where Satyavan lay, she saw him struggling to get up. Gently placing her hands below his head, she helped him sit up. Satyavan smiled. That smile meant so much to her. He lay down and placed his head on her lap once again. In a feeble voice he queried, 'Did I sleep for too long? Why did you not wake me up? I saw a dark person dragging me away with a rope. Was it all a dream? I even saw you conversing with him intensely. Did I hallucinate…'

 *Between dreams and memories is sometimes a dark reality.*

Savitri stroked his head and smiled. 'You did indeed sleep for too long. Everything is all right now. If you have the strength to stand up, let's go back home now. It's very late already. If you can manage to stand up, let us return. I will explain everything to you tomorrow morning.'

Holding Satyavan tightly, Savitri began their return journey through the dark woods. Using a nearby forest fire as an indicator of their path, the loving couple retraced their way home. In the meanwhile, the blind Dyumatsena suddenly saw an intense flash of light coming through a small window in the hermitage and the next instant his eyesight was restored. Along with the happiness of the miracle, the old king and his wife began to worry about the safety of their son who was destined to die that night. They ran out of the hermitage and began searching in the vicinity for their son and daughter-in-law. Seeing their desperation and their grief, many sages gathered around the elderly couple, trying to pacify them.

Just then, round the corner, they saw the silhouette of two people huddled together walking towards them. As they reached closer, Dyumatsena cried out, 'Satyavan! My son, you are alive!'

As the old parents embraced their only son, Savitri respectfully stood a little distance away, shedding tears of joy. A great and powerful sage named Gautama Rishi stepped towards them. 'As long as Savitri is by Satyavan's side, nothing can go wrong with him. Satyavan, you are indeed fortunate that you have a wife like Savitri. It is only through Savitri's determination to save your life and maintain this relationship for life that you are still alive. I want Savitri to narrate everything that happened in the forest to everyone assembled here for posterity's sake. This story is a story of how the determination to stay in a relationship can keep the relationship alive through the biggest of obstacles and calamities. This is a story of the power of goodwill. This is a story of the power of love.'

❁ *Determination to stay in a relationship will eventually manifest as satisfaction in the relationship.*

As Savitri narrated the incident that took place in the forest, everyone was amazed at the amount of determination that Savitri had displayed to save Satyavan. So much so that she was ready to face the god of death himself. She had literally snatched Satyavan from the jaws of death and brought him back to life. She saved a relationship from imminent death.

Satyavan and Savitri lived happily ever after. But the story of her determination lived much longer than them...

❁ *While science is trying so hard to save humans from death, it is to be wished that we try hard enough to save our relationships from death.*

THE DETERMINATION TO STAY TOGETHER

When the going gets tough, the easiest option is to give up. A relationship is like hiking up a steep mountain. No one reaches the summit of a mountain by giving up when faced with the first obstacle. There are many reasons not to stay together but the one reason to not give up is love. And that's enough of a reason to deal with all the obstacles that arise on the hike up the mountain of any relationship. Determination means doing what's necessary even when it seems difficult. Determination allows us to act even when we don't know how to. Determination gives us courage. The mind automatically generates internal resources that are needed to overcome resistance, setbacks and self-doubt, given enough determination and will.

This was the story of Satyavan and Savitri who loved each other more than anything else in the world. It was so intense that obstacles simply melted away in front of their love. During the difficult times in relationships, each person has to endeavour to keep things going. In this story, Savitri was resolute not to let go of the relationship even in the face of death itself. Her determination arose in the form of various ideas that inspired her to convince death itself. When there is determination to continue a relationship, you will be able to access a data bank of ways to deal with the obstacles that you stumble upon. In her desperation to save Satyavan, Savitri was saying things that she didn't realise she knew.

Ordinary relationships transform into extraordinary bonds when ordinary people show extraordinary determination. Do not underestimate the role of determination in a relationship. History never remembers those who ventured into something and gave up when faced with difficulties. History is not about extraordinary people. It's about ordinary people who showed extraordinary determination for a cause. Most people either run away from fears and disappointments or sheepishly agree to become their captives. Determined people choose to face them. Determination is all about intention. Once the lenses of intention are clean, no obstacle no matter how big it may be, seems insurmountable when viewed through them. Instead of complaining, determined people begin to explore ways of dealing with the situation realistically. For those who possess grit, 'NO' reads like 'ON'. Grit empowers while fear paralyses.

Savitri wasn't extraordinary. She was an ordinary woman who exhibited such extraordinary determination that posterity celebrates her grit even today. She could have ended the relationship before it even began because she knew the hurdles that lay ahead of her, but rather than running away from her fears or sheepishly becoming a passive captive to them, Savitri decided to face them. She made her intention very clear from the beginning to herself. Discarding the selfishness that prompted her to think about her own life and future, she decided to focus on the future of her love for Satyavan. Though everyone around her, including her father and the wise sage Narada, discouraged her from jumping into this potentially short-lived relationship, she decided to stick it out and fight fate itself.

Choices are the greatest enemy of determination. When there are various choices available, the mind inevitably takes the easy route. The subconscious mind is always scanning for easy and less cumbersome ways of dealing with the difficulties that arise in relationships. If you spend even one moment considering an alternative, the mind will latch on to it immediately. Therefore, rather than putting your full energy and potential into making a relationship work in the long term, the mind will look for short-term gains and not want to think too far. Determination forces one to prioritise the long-term implications of every choice one makes. Determination is the enemy of options. Many prefer to change relationships like the channels on a television set. Those who are determined to commit themselves to a relationship for life understand that there is great benefit in limiting one's choices. They understand that if someone is not satisfied with one person, they will never be satisfied with anyone. No matter how many channels you keep changing, the satisfaction your mind is searching for will prove elusive. The determination to stick to one relationship actually increases the overall levels of happiness and contentment in a human being.

Savitri's father asked her to make a wise choice. She had many options, being such a beautiful princess at the peak of her life. Why did she have to choose Satyavan, who was meant to die in a year's time? Isn't it foolish to choose the worst when you could have the best? Savitri realised that good and bad are a matter of chance and not choice. Should she choose a life of ease, or a life of satisfaction? No matter what choice you make in life, there will always be difficulties. No difficulty means no life. She knew that finding satisfaction in the midst of complications is the real art of living. She had made her choice and was determined to stick to it. For her, a few moments spent with Satyavan were more meaningful and satisfying than a million moments spent with someone her heart didn't connect with. Just because a rose and a thorn spend their life together, it doesn't mean they have a very rosy life.

Love that is temporary cannot belong to the soul, which is permanent. The human commitments that last are always connected at the level of the soul. When two people commit to one another, the question to be asked is: what are they willing to do to grow together? Commitment to another begins when you commit to yourself. It simply means being ready to grow in every way possible in order to connect wholeheartedly with the person you love. Relationships grow when people grow. We cannot expect relationships to grow when we ourselves are not ready to bring about consistent positive transformation in our attitudes and mindsets. When two people are committed to one another, they need to be determined to grow in order to stay true to their commitments. Love brings awareness of good qualities and time brings awareness of bad qualities. In time, when the bad qualities become visible in the people you love, most people become critical of their once idealised relationship. The moment contempt finds its way into a relationship, it begins to evaporate. In order to stop oneself from venturing into the abrasive zone of criticism, one has to commit to oneself. Commitment to one's own growth brings commitment to the growth of the relationship.

Savitri's love for Satyavan wasn't at the level of the body. If it was, then she would be a fool to marry someone who wasn't going to survive for long. Savitri showed us the real meaning of the word 'soulmate'. Her commitment to Satyavan manifested itself as commitment to her own growth. She knew that if she had to handle the imminent calamity in their lives, she had to be well-equipped. For one year, along with showing her commitment to loving Satyavan, she spent time pursuing self-growth. For her self-growth meant strengthening herself internally and emotionally in various ways. She knew that Satyavan had a plethora of good qualities but one shortcoming. It wasn't a shortcoming that could be ignored as trivial. It was a serious issue. But Savitri realised that if she focussed on that aspect of Satyavan's fate, it would manifest itself either in the form of an accusation during a quarrel or it would be expressed as a negative vibration that would harm their connection. She assiduously worked on her attitude and mindset so nothing would impede their relationship in a subtle or overt way.

The world is filled with people who are determined to be critical. Lasting love is about having the determination to be kind. We tend to be kind to everyone in the world except to the people we love the most. The natural tendency is to take the people closest to you for granted. Kindness is like a muscle that has to be exercised every day. There are many people who claim to be in love but have never ever used the kindness muscle. Relationships grow when people are determined to be kind to one another.

The love of Satyavan and Savitri was so strong that even death couldn't separate them. What could be a greater threat to a relationship than death itself? Like death there are many reasons that separate two people, including doubts, ambitions, differences of opinion, taste, nature, horoscope mismatch, and so on. The one factor that can help two people overcome all these obstacles and make a relationship last a lifetime is determination.

Chapter 5.5

A CONDITION ABOUT CONDITIONS

'How do you manage five husbands when we are struggling with just one?' Krishna's wife, Satyabhama, enquired sincerely of the wife of the five Pandavas. Satyabhama had always wanted to ask her this question, especially after hearing so many anecdotes from so many sources about her odd but happy married life.

'Conditions!' pat came Draupadi's reply.

'How can conditions be the reason for a happy marriage? I always thought that conditions strangle relationships. And here you say that the secret of your happy marriage is conditions.' Satyabhama was visibly taken aback by Draupadi's one-word answer. She knew that there must be more than she had comprehended in that single word, uttered by the one woman she knew who had managed to survive a difficult marriage. Not just survived but thrived. Of course what she had gone through were not just difficulties but catastrophes. In spite of that, not once did she have any disagreements or fights with her husbands. Was she just another woman who had decided to tolerate whatever her husbands did just to ensure that the marriage survived? Gauging Draupadi's fiercely determined nature, Satyabhama knew that it couldn't be true.

❁ *If a condition makes the condition of the relationship better then it's a good condition, but if it worsens the condition of the relationship then it's a bad condition.*

Seeing the confusion on her friend's beautiful face, Draupadi decided to elaborate on her statement with a series of stories. She knew that these stories that she had heard from Narada Muni had transformed her life and her relationships with her husbands. She knew that anyone hearing how these stories had shaped her own story would soon be able to weave a success story of their own. Satyabhama sat beside Draupadi, holding her hand as she dived into these love stories, each of which surprisingly took place in just one family—the family of Draupadi's husbands.

❁ *Old stories help you create new stories without making the old mistakes.*

❧

He was a man obsessively in love. Actually it was frustrated love. He roamed the forest aimlessly. Dishevelled hair, unkempt beard, dirty clothes and torn footwear became the characteristics of Pururava. A king had become a beggar because of a woman. He was begging for love. He was begging for attention. He was begging for just one glance from his beloved. Someone he had dedicated his life to had left him for two lambs … of all things, lambs!

❁ *When you beg for love, all you get are pennies.*

No one begs for diamonds, only for pennies.

Pururava's love was actually madness. Nothing short of madness. He was madly in love with the apsara Urvashi and had been so from the moment he had first set his eyes on her.

It was a moonlit night. When the full moon glistened in the skies, Pururava would look for love. His romantic mood bloomed with the moon. This was probably because he was born in the lunar dynasty, and was the grandson of the moon-god. As he was galloping back from a hunting expedition, the skies darkened. The moon rose. In the dark woods, he saw a flash of white. The striking contrast caught his attention. He moved in that direction on his horse. What he saw there changed the course of his life forever.

There she was dressed in silken white garments that shone as brilliantly as moonlight. Seated on a rock in the most tantalising manner, Urvashi appeared like a star fallen to the ground. Pururava's eyes were glued to her, her smile stirring his passion. He instantly decided that this was the angel he had been waiting for all his life. He had no idea who she was or what she was doing in such a god-forsaken place at this hour. All he knew was that he was bowled over by her beauty. He was ready to go to any lengths to make her his own.

As he inched closer to this dazzling beauty, he could hear her singing. Every word of the song that emanated from her rosy lips was like nectar oozing from a flower. Her voice further mesmerised him. She was singing of her hankering for true love. In that instant Pururava became convinced that he would be the one to fulfil her longing.

❁ *The love that arouses hankering is not a love that will bring fulfilment.*

Subjected to a strange curse, Urvashi had descended from her heavenly abode to spend a stipulated few years on the earthly plane. As soon as she landed, she had set her sights upon Pururava. His handsome face and graceful demeanour had sparked her interest. Having mastered the art of seduction, Urvashi attracted Pururava towards herself. Seeing him go crazy over her beauty, she realised that he would be an ideal partner for her while she was on earth.

Falling to his knees, Pururava held her hand. With teary eyes and a sincere look, Pururava spoke his heart, 'O princess of my dreams, I don't know who you are. I don't know where you have come from. But I do know that I have become a slave to your beauty. Your smiles control me now and your voice binds me. I am Pururava, the king of this land. Become my queen and I will keep you happy. I assure you heaven on earth. The creator surely exhausted all his creativity after creating a masterpiece like you. There can't be anyone more beautiful than you in all the three worlds. Become mine and I will bathe you in my love.'

❁ *You can either be bound by love or be free to love. When love binds you, it frustrates you. When love frees you, it uplifts you.*

With a shy smile, Urvashi replied, 'Who would not want to marry a handsome king like you? I must say I am impressed with your confidence. No one has ever proposed to me like this. All I seek is love. I am sure that you are as good at winning in love as in winning at war. I do want to bask in your love. But …'

❁ *In relationships every 'but' is followed by a selfish concern.*

'Tell me your concern. I will allay it immediately. Let there be no secrets between us. Please share your concerns and I will take care of them,' Pururava immediately replied.

'I have three conditions for this marriage to happen,' Urvashi stated.

'Even if you have a million conditions, I am ready to fulfil them if they will help me attain you.' Pururava was confident in his ability to fulfil all her demands.

❁ *When requests become demands, love becomes pain.*

'If you are so sure then here they are. The first condition is that you have to take care of my two pet lambs. The second condition is that you will only feed me food that is cooked in pure ghee. The third condition is that you will never appear naked in front of any one, including me. You can unite with me in the dark, but never in the light.' Urvashi spelled out her conditions clearly in a very serious manner.

A smile appeared on Pururava's face on hearing her apparently silly conditions. In a moment, that smile turned into a giggle and suddenly into a laugh. In a few seconds, Pururava was laughing hysterically, rolling on the ground. Urvashi was irritated at his behaviour. She told him if he didn't take her conditions seriously she would leave. Pururava sobered up but he still couldn't believe what he had heard. Whoever had heard of marriage on condition that the partner should take care of a couple of pets? It seemed too stupid. However, perceiving how serious Urvashi was about these conditions, Pururava decided to drop the matter and agree to anything she asked.

❁ *What seems seriously silly to one is taken seriously by another. Perceptions seriously alter realities.*

Very soon the two were united in a marital bond. Their love soared. Pururava could not have enough of her. No matter how many hours he spent in her loving company, it just wasn't enough. Of course the two pets were always hanging around, irritating him on occasion. But he learnt to accept the package. Years passed as if in a moment. Urvashi always remained next to him, loving him in ways that he had never experienced before.

❁ *Love is a beautiful gift which is often packed in complex packaging. Don't get entangled with the packaging, reach for the gift.*

One day something happened that shook the foundation on which this relationship was built. Indra started missing the ravishing presence of Urvashi in the heavens. Noting that the stipulated time of her residence on the earthly plane was nearing completion, he appointed the Gandharvas to undertake the mission of bringing back the heartthrob of the heavens.

In order to bring her back, the Gandharvas realised that they would have to create friction between the partners. They chose the simplest means of creating a divergence. Break the conditions!

❁ *Dividers devise ideas to divide people to gain dividends for themselves.*

They chose a time when Pururava was immersed in loving Urvashi intensely. While the lovers were absorbed in each other, the Gandharvas grabbed the lambs and fled. As they were taking off, the two lambs began to bleat loudly. Their screams instantly roused Urvashi. Pushing her husband off, Urvashi chastised him for being careless. She became quite hysterical at her pets were being kidnapped. She began to push Pururava. Shoving him off the bed, she beat him on his shoulders. Pururava was initially confused and then began to panic realising the gravity of the situation. The future of his marriage was dependent on the safety of those lambs. Desperate to salvage the situation, he ran out of the bedroom, picking up a sword on his way out. Urvashi rushed out behind him.

❁ *Panicking is like diving into the water; you can't breathe till you come out.*

Thinking is connected with breathing. When you cannot breathe steadily, you cannot think clearly. Similarly, in a state of panic, you cannot think steadily.

Just as Pururava stepped out of the palace to follow the fleeing Gandharvas, there was a flash of lightning across the skies, orchestrated by Indra. A loud gasp followed. Numerous guards, maids and attendants stood with their hands covering their mouths and their eyes wide open. Pururava looked around puzzled. What was the reason for their shock? Suddenly, he realised the reason!

A feeling of intense shame swept over him as he tried to cover his naked body that had been fully exposed by the cleverly orchestrated lightning spell by the king of the heavens. Urvashi was shocked. He had broken two of her conditions at once. She felt devastated. She took off and threw away her wedding ring, and glared at Pururava in great anger.

Having accomplished the purpose of their mission, the Gandharvas dropped the lambs and escaped. Pururava sheepishly ran towards the lambs. He gathered them in his arms and using them to cover himself, walked up to his disgusted wife. Handing over the two lambs to her, he stood with his head lowered.

Taking the two lambs from her husband, Urvashi felt like she was taking her life back. She loved those two lambs more than life itself. Reminding Pururava that he had broken two of her conditions, Urvashi decided to leave him and return to her heavenly home.

'When you cannot even protect my lambs, how can you protect me? I told you that you should never appear unclothed in front of others or even in front of me in the light. Are the conditions I placed too onerous? Did I ask for the heavens? Did I ask for unlimited wealth? Did I ask for power, position or control? I asked you for such small, innocent things and you failed to keep those conditions. What kind of a man are you? I am grateful to you for all the love you have given me, but I have reciprocated your love in multiples of the emotion you showered on me. Now it's time to part. My conditions apply now.'

❁ *Sometimes the hole is small and the thread is big and at other times the hole is big and the thread is small.*

Sometimes when conditions are small and your abilities are big, it's much more difficult to fulfil them rather than when the conditions are big and your abilities are small.

Pururava begged and pleaded but Urvashi sailed out of the palace and ascended to the heavens with her pets. The devastated king cried out in agony. His pain mattered not a bit to Urvashi anymore. She had moved on, her past forgotten in a moment. Her conditions were more important to her than his condition. The marriage was based on her conditions and non-compliance with the conditions broke the conditional marriage.

 *When your conditions are more important than the condition of the person you love, then your love is in a very bad condition.*

~

'I can't believe that within this innocent-looking sweet person is hidden a sinister serial killer.' King Shantanu was following his wife for the seventh consecutive time.

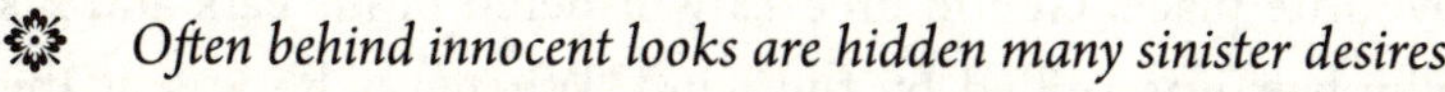

Often behind innocent looks are hidden many sinister desires.

The seven years they had been married were simultaneously the best and the worst times of his life. Ganga was the sweetest person he had ever met. The most sensitive woman he had ever come across in his life. Her gentle behaviour and caring nature had won his heart. Not only did she take wonderful care of him, but also of his subjects. She was a true mother to the kingdom. A queen they all had begun to worship as a mother.

Though she had that adorable aspect, she also had this reprehensible side. Shantanu had kept this secret side of Ganga hidden from the world. For seven consecutive years he had tolerated a pain that only a father who sees his child dying right in front of his eyes can understand. Every year the pain only increased as a new pain was added to the pain inflicted in the previous year.

When you love one side of a person you are a lover, when you hate one side of a person you are a spouse, and when you love both sides of a person you are a saint.

Shantanu still remembered their first meeting vividly. In fact, they had met in the exact same spot he was standing on right now. But the atmosphere at that time was different. Very different. It wasn't hot and humid as it was now. It wasn't harsh and cruel. Not only was the outer environment barbarous but even the inner environment of Shantanu's heart was devastated. There was no peace inside and no peace outside anymore. But it had been different back then. The day he had met his beloved Ganga had been a magical day—

It was the twilight hour. The king's favourite time at his favourite place. Gentle breezes whispered in his ears and his silky hair was ruffled by the wind. Whenever he was at the river bank, seated on this rock overlooking the massive river, the experience he had was profound. As he was admiring the graceful dance of the river, something unbelievable happened. A beautiful maiden, the like of whom he had never seen in his life, arose right from the middle of the river. His heart skipped a beat as his eyes gazed at the delicate fairy sashaying across the surface of the water towards him. She was walking over the waters almost as if she were walking on land.

Walking up to the king, the dazzling beauty sat on his lap straightaway. The king was shocked at her audacity. Her soft, supple body sent a shiver down his spine. His skin broke out in gooseflesh and his hair follicles stood upright. He had to close his eyes to savour the experience. He had no idea who this divine lady was. But whoever she was, she had managed to capture his heart in a way no other woman ever had. He placed his chin on her shoulders and rested against her. Slowly he curved his arms around her waist and held her in a secure grip. Only when she laughed did he come out of his trance. Realising what he had just done, he loosened his arms and looked into her deep blue eyes. It seemed as if he was looking into the depths of an azure river.

Her rosy lips moved and uttered a few words that he couldn't even hear, as lost as he was. She placed her hands on his shoulders to shake him a little. When she was sure that she had his attention, Ganga began to speak. 'O King Shantanu, do not think I am a stranger. I am an integral part of your life in many ways. Know me to be Ganga, the goddess of the river you so admire. Your father had promised me on this very spot that you would be my husband. I have been waiting ever since for our union. O King, please accept me.'

Shantanu was flattered by this bold proposal. Who would not want to marry a goddess? Most men hope to have a wife who looks like a goddess and here was a goddess who hoped to be his wife. Somewhere in his heart he knew that nothing so good comes without a condition. As soon as he nodded his agreement, she revealed what it was.

❁ *In the corner of every beautiful advertisement is a cleverly hidden condition. This is true with marketing and more so with a wedding.*

'I have a condition for this marriage.' On hearing her say that Shantanu smiled.

He asked her to express what was on her mind. Ganga told him that unlimited trust should be the foundation of their relationship. Even if he found every reason to doubt her intention, he should never doubt it in spite of her questionable actions. Though Shantanu found this condition to be a difficult one, he still wanted to acquiesce with it due to his infatuation with the goddess.

Very soon Ganga had become the centre of his life. Everything in his life revolved around her. She managed to touch the hearts of anyone who met her even once. Everything was more than perfect for a year. Then it happened!

After delivering a child most women would have to rest for a few hours at least. Not Ganga. She was made of different stuff. As soon as she delivered the baby, she got up and began to walk away from the palace with the baby in her hands. By that time someone had informed King Shantanu of the good news of the birth of a baby boy. He reached just in time to see Ganga walking out of the palace with the child in her arms. He was so surprised, he silently followed her, all the way to the riverside. What he saw there shocked him to the core!

His gentle and kind-hearted wife threw their newborn child into the river as if she had discarded some garbage. Not looking back even once, she walked away from the riverbank. No trace of sadness or agitation could be seen on her beautiful, serene face. Shantanu was completely bewildered by this cruel, inhuman act. He was shattered by the loss of his first-born. He hadn't even got a chance to gaze at the smiling face of his baby. A father's heart was crying out to reach for the baby which had been just thrown into the waters. However, by the time he reached the spot, the currents had swept the child away too far out of his reach.

When he returned to the palace, Ganga behaved as if nothing had happened. She was going about her activities as if it was a normal day. The nine months of pregnancy, the labour pains and the delivery seemed to have been wiped out from her memory. She didn't even refer to the birth of the child. Shantanu was completely confused about this behaviour. He desperately wanted to confront her and ask her about her peculiar action, but he remembered her condition and decided to stay quiet.

 *How long will there be a gap between what you feel and what you say and between what you say and what you actually mean to say?*

In a few days, the pain of the loss waned. The love his wife showered on him made it easier to forget the traumatic episode. In a few weeks Ganga was pregnant again and new hope arose in the king's mind. Exactly a year after the first incident, Ganga gave birth to another son. The excited king came running to the palace only to see her walk out with the newborn child in her arms. In great anguish he followed her. History repeated itself and her cruelty prevailed. Dumping her child into the river, she made her way back to the palace and behaved as if nothing had happened.

Every year after that, for the next five years, the same sequence of events was repeated. Every year Shantanu saw Ganga throw their newborn child into the river. After losing seven children one after the other, Shantanu became highly disturbed. The eighth time that Ganga walked up to the river to throw the child into the water, Shantanu tugged at her shoulders and yanked the child away from her.

'What are you doing, you cruel woman? How can a mother be so demonic as to kill her own children? I have been observing you silently for the last seven years. I didn't utter a single word as my heart screamed in pain to see you throw our children into this river one by one. But I can't bear it anymore. Why are you doing this? All year long you are so loving and gentle, how can you be so violently cruel once a year? Are you a witch? Are you a sadist who derives pleasure from others' pain? Who are you?'

❁ *Suppressing emotions is like lighting the fuse of a stick of dynamite. Sometimes the fuse lasts for years. But when the fire reaches the end of the fuse, there is always an explosion. Thus suppression is simply delayed explosion.*

Ganga smiled at him. She had guessed that this was coming. 'O King, I had mentioned to you right at the beginning that the basis of this relationship has to be trust.'

'That doesn't mean you can kill our children like this,' Shantanu argued with great anger. He was trembling with rage.

Ganga was poised and didn't appear disturbed by his anger. She said, 'I had told you that the condition for this marriage was that you would not doubt my intentions even if my actions seem apparently wrong.'

'I tolerated your cruel actions seven times. I cannot subdue the feelings of a wronged father any longer. I need to know the reason for your inhuman action at any cost.' Shantanu knew that this question could cost him the relationship itself. But at this point mental peace was more important for him than any relationship. How long could he be with a woman who had such sinister motives? How could there be such a ghastly personality hidden beneath such a beautiful face?

❁ *When hearts are at war for too long, you are ready to pay any price for peace.*

'Okay, if you want to know, I will tell you everything. Every time I threw our child into the river, I would whisper into the ears of the baby that this was for his own good. When the baby would hear that every one of them smiled. Since you are of human origin, you are only concerned about actions in this life. But since I am of the higher realms, I know about many previous lives and to quite an extent about future lives as well. These eight children born to us were the eight Vasus in their previous lives. It so happened that they along with their wives were enjoying themselves on the peaks of Mount Meru. One of their wives spotted Nandini, the wish-fulfilling cow of Sage Vashishta. She became obsessed with possessing that cow. After pestering her husband Dyu for a long time, she managed to convince him to fetch her the cow.'

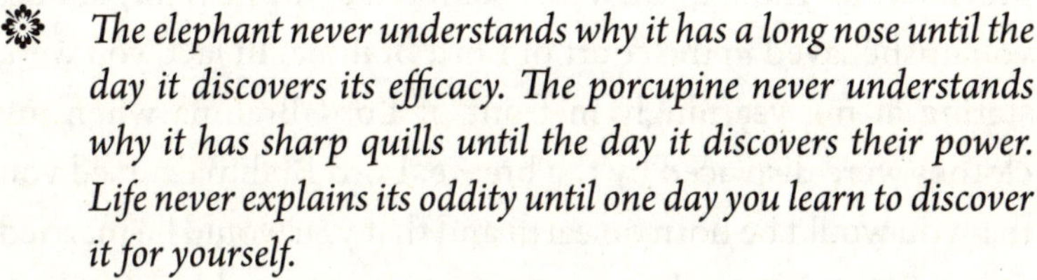

The elephant never understands why it has a long nose until the day it discovers its efficacy. The porcupine never understands why it has sharp quills until the day it discovers their power. Life never explains its oddity until one day you learn to discover it for yourself.

'Knowing fully well the consequence of meddling with a powerful sage like Vashishta, Dyu along with his brothers dragged the cow away from the ashram while the sage was away. When the sage returned and learnt of the theft, he at once cursed the eight Vasus, condemning them to be born as greedy humans, who were always eyeing others' property. When the Vasus begged for forgiveness, the sage's heart softened. As an addendum to his curse, he said that the seven Vasus who were co-conspirators would take birth in human society, but after suffering the pangs of being restricted to a mother's womb and the pain of childbirth, they would return to their celestial abodes. However, since Dyu was the one who had actively planned the notorious crime, he would have to suffer for an entire lifetime. No one was ready to mother these eight Vasus, knowing of the magnitude of the curse and of the highly temporary nature of the associated motherhood. I agreed to take on the thankless task of being their mother and helping them get free of their curse.'

 *While you are busy over-valuing what others have, you are busy under-valuing what you have.*

'In accordance with this curse, I was not killing the seven children; rather I was liberating them from the earthly plane of suffering and reinstating them in their heavenly positions and reuniting them with their waiting wives. As far as you are concerned, you were the great King Mahabhisha in your previous life. Though you were promoted to the heavenly abode, you misbehaved in the court of Lord Brahma. In fact, you were staring at me yearningly in front of Lord Brahma when my clothes were displaced by the breeze. Lord Brahma cursed you that you would be born on earth and that you would be married to me. Though your desire to unite with me would be fulfilled, Brahma cursed you that you would never experience pleasure in my company. Rather, my actions would always leave you mentally disturbed.'

'Now tell me O king, where was I at fault in the whole affair? I was neither responsible for the actions of your sons nor for your actions in your previous life. In spite of that, I got dragged into doing something that I would never ever want to do. That is why I had warned you right at the beginning never to doubt my intentions even if there is every reason to doubt my actions. Now that my intentions have been doubted, my condition will prevail. I hereby leave you with your son.'

The marriage was based on her condition and non-compliance with the condition broke the conditional marriage. Her condition was unconditional trust in her intentions. Her actions had made his condition in life so pathetic that he became blind to her condition.

❁ *Unconditional love can flow only when unconditional trust is earned.*

'Why couldn't I smell her selfishness? Why did I only smell her fragrance?' Shantanu's mind was in turmoil. He had to decide once again if he wanted to enter a new relationship based on a condition. Two decades ago one conditional relationship had ended in a mess. It had taken him all these years to recover. He had no energy left to enter into another messy relationship that began with a condition.

❁ *Messy relationships are those you decide to pursue while ignoring the warning of your intuition.*

King Shantanu had been out on a hunting expedition. He carefully avoided going close to the River Ganga to sidestep the flood of memories of the goddess he loved and hated simultaneously. Suddenly he caught a scent. Wafting through the cool breeze was a fragrance that was more heavenly than anything he had ever experienced. Immediately halting his horse, the king got off and began to walk towards the source of the divine fragrance. He didn't know what to expect. Maybe a flower, maybe a fruit, maybe some exotic animal like the musk deer, maybe ... of course he knew it couldn't be any of these things. He had enough experience to understand that this was different from any regular smell. This was divine, beyond anything earthly.

❁ *A bad relationship is one-sided like a fragrance that spreads only in the direction of the wind.*

A good relationship is like fame, it spreads in every direction.

As he stepped out into a clearing, he saw something that stunned him. In front of him, a few feet away, was the most exquisitely beautiful fisherwoman seated on a boat, with her back towards him. Even though he couldn't see her face, everything about her indicated that this was the most beautiful girl in all of creation. As he moved towards her, his intelligence screamed, 'Not again!' This was definitely a trap, his brain warned him. But his heart took charge and dragged his feet along.

✿ *Falling in love after a bad experience is always a tug of war between a doubtful head and a stubborn heart.*

Soon he was standing right next to her boat. Sensing someone's presence behind her, the fisherwoman turned around. Shantanu almost fainted. Gorgeous would be an understatement to describe her beauty. This girl was stunningly beautiful. Flawlessly created by God. Observing his stupefied state, the girl smiled shyly. She was flattered by his expression. Her smile made her even more beautiful. His knees wobbled. He had to sit down. Sitting on the edge of the boat, he kept staring at her openly.

By the style of his clothes and the value of the ornaments that adorned his body, she could ascertain that he was royalty. Not wanting to offend him but at the same time wanting to get away from his embarrassing stare, she shook the boat. The sudden rocking of the boat shook him out of his reverie. He spoke with a gentle, loving voice, quite uncharacteristic of him. In doing so, he surprised himself. In the last two decades he hadn't heard himself speak like that. 'O delicate lady, please know me to be King Shantanu of the prestigious Bharata dynasty. O divinely fragrant one, please tell me, who are you?'

✿ *A note is about what you say.*
A tone is about how you say it.
The tone is always more important than the note.

Realising the stature of the person standing before her, she replied shyly, 'O great king, I am Satyavati, the daughter of the leader of the fishermen community. I live in a village close by, in my father's care.'

Her eyes spoke so much. Her mannerisms spoke so much. More than anything else, her fragrance spoke so much. All the desires that Shantanu had subdued for so many years burst forth like a volcano erupting uncontrollably. Now his doubtful head played no further role in the affair. He shoved it away as he took her hand in his. 'Will you marry me?'

❁ *When desires dictate your intelligence, it's called noise.*
When intelligence rides your desires, it's called choice.

He couldn't believe that he had actually said it. She blushed, her cheeks instantly turning a bright red. She lowered her head to hide her smile. Then she looked up shyly into his eyes and said, 'I will comply with my father's decision. If he agrees then I would be honoured to be your wife.'

The king got up, determined to make her his. Asking her to lead him to her dwelling, he began to follow her. Her father was totally taken aback when the king of the land came into his humble dwelling. How does one compare the head of a fishing community to the head of a kingdom? Satyavati's father went into a state of disbelief and shock. After running around and shouting out a few orders to his men to arrange a respectable welcome for the king, he rushed back to be with the king. Not knowing what to do or what to say, he behaved quite awkwardly.

Understanding the embarrassment the sudden entry of a king had caused in the fishing community, Shantanu smiled. Touching Satyavati's father's shoulder, Shantanu asked him to relax. Making do with the simple seat that was available, he made the elder fisherman also sit close by. Without mincing any words, the king asked for Satyavati's hand in marriage. He told the shocked father that his heart was set on his beautiful daughter and he wanted to marry no one else but her. The kingdom had lacked a queen for a long time, the citizens needed a mother and the king needed a companion. Satyavati's father did not know whether to cry or to laugh. The old man's reaction made Shantanu feel confident about the alliance.

❁ *Life keeps sending surprises; it's up to us to convert them into either disappointments or opportunities.*

'I am okay with the marriage but I have a condition.' The word 'condition' coming from the mouth of the father sent a tremor down Shantanu's spine. He hated that word from the core of his being. He glared at the father, who looked back with a cold stare. His humble and simple demeanour was gone, replaced with the stern and determined look of a businessman who had the upper hand in the transaction. The king was aghast. How could a person change so drastically? The marriage proposal had become a business proposal. Without waiting for the king's reply, he continued, 'My condition is that the son born to my daughter should be the next king.'

The angered king stood up. The rickety seat toppled over behind him. 'Impossible! My first son Devavrata has already been anointed as heir to the throne of Hastinapur. I cannot agree to your condition. More than anything else I hate relationships that are based on conditions. Satyavati, do you agree with what your father says? Just tell me that you don't and I will take you with me no matter who opposes us. Your word will decide the fate of our relationship.'

Understanding the gravity of the situation, Satyavati spoke from her heart, 'My father is my greatest well-wisher. If he has decided that this is to be his condition for the marriage, then I will abide by it. Moreover, a girl who goes alone to another house needs such conditions to protect her from envious elements. The only true support for a girl is her son and it's her duty to strengthen his position from the beginning.'

The king abruptly walked out of the house. He walked out of the community and out into the countryside. But he could not walk out of his desire for Satyavati. It almost felt like he had left his heart on the boat on which she was seated when he had first seen her. It was still rocking...

❁ *Only when you try walking out of something do you realise how much you are bound by it.*

No matter how much he tried to forget her, her smile haunted him. Days passed into weeks, but the maddening effect of her smile continued. The king was torn between his heart and his intelligence. His heart told him to agree while his intelligence warned him never to agree. His heart told him that as a queen she had every right to ask for this and his intelligence told him this was history repeating itself. His heart told him that the relationship is more important than any condition and his intelligence told him that a condition had already ruined a previous relationship and now another condition would surely ruin this one.

❁ *To win an inner duel, you have to first accept that your heart is at war.*

Neglecting his royal duties, he chose to remain in solitary confinement, trying to soothe his troubled heart. When

Devavrata, his eighth son, born of Ganga, came to know of his father's condition, rather than confronting his father, he decided to go to the root of the problem.

❁ *To reach the root of problems you have to dig deep into the soil of the heart.*

Very soon he was standing in front of Satyavati and her father. Describing his father's condition to them, Devavrata requested them to explain. He told them that his father had remained silent from the moment he came back from their house. No one including the ministers knew what the issue was. Satyavati bluntly said, 'The issue is you!'

Devavrata was shocked to hear that. But keeping his hurt feelings aside he focussed on the problem at hand. He asked her how he could be the issue when he didn't even know about what had transpired. Satyavati's father explained the dilemma to Devavrata, who simply smiled on hearing of the pettiness of the matter. He said the matter was so simple that it could have been solved in a moment. The surprised father-daughter duo questioned him about the import of his statement.

❁ *The most complicated problem is the one in which you are the problem.*

He said, 'The solution is very simple. I hereby take a solemn vow that I will never sit on the throne of Hastinapur. There, that solves the problem.'

Satyavati's father said, 'What if your sons demand their rights over the throne? What would my grandsons do then?'

Devavrata was disgusted at their pettiness. He never thought that someone could be so greedy as to be willing to mess up a present relationship for a relationship that didn't even exist. How could they demand the throne for a child of a child who was yet to be born? It seemed nothing less than madness. But that's not how they saw it. They saw this conditional deal as an assurance of security for their future. It is often the case that when different people see the same situation with different perspectives, they actually see different things.

Deciding not to argue with people who didn't seem logically oriented and also not wanting to arm-twist destiny, Devavrata decided to deal with the current problem first. The future would no doubt deal with itself later. Right now what mattered the most to him was his father's happiness. It was obvious to him that his father's happiness depended on his relationship with Satyavati. He decided to completely focus on that and dedicate his life, happiness and choices to usher in that happiness. Devavrata then did something that had never happened in the history of the Kshatriya clan.

 *Instead of worrying about the white hair that hasn't grown, one should focus on preserving the black hair that hasn't gone.*

Instead of worrying about a problem that hasn't begun, one should focus on stabilising the situation at hand.

'Keeping the sun, the moon, the stars, the directions, air, water, earth, ether and the paramatma as my witness, I, Devavrata, the son of Ganga and Shantanu, take this vow that I will never ascend the throne of Hastinapur and I will never get married.' As soon as Devavrata took the vow, there was tremendous uproar in the universe. From all directions only one sound could be heard—

'Bhishma! Bhishma!'

Satyavati and her father realised the gravity of his vow only then. Bhishma meant one who has taken a terrible vow. They had made him take this vow unknowingly. Something told the father-daughter duo that though they had accomplished what they had set out to do, since they had troubled such noble souls through this condition of theirs, they would never experience the fruits of their plan.

❁ *When you begin your life together by stepping on others' toes, you are actually trampling on your peace. Harassing others boomerangs into self-harassment.*

The marriage did happen. Satyavati did have two sons. Bhishma never ascended the throne and neither did he ever get married. Though Shantanu was happy to unite with Satyavati, he lived with great guilt in his heart that he had let his son Devavrata down. That guilt nibbled at his heart constantly and drained the vitality from his life. With the passing of Shantanu, his oldest son, Chitrangada, ascended the throne, but died shortly thereafter due to a petty quarrel with the Gandharvas. His second son, Vichitravirya, who then ascended the throne, also died very soon of an ailment. The dramatis personae left were Satyavati and the result of her condition, Bhishma.

The throne remained empty though her condition prevailed. Her condition had won her a relationship but had taken away all the joy connected with it.

❁ *You may win in your conditions but you then lose in your relationship.*

'Wow! What stories! Hearing these three stories has made me feel that any condition will break a relationship eventually.' Satyabhama was visibly affected by the tales and the way conditions had destroyed the relationships between people who loved each other.

Draupadi immediately spoke up, not wanting her to completely dismiss the importance of conditions in making relationships work. 'There are two types of conditions. There are negative conditions and there are positive conditions. All the examples I described so far were negative conditions that destroy relationships.'

✿ *Everything good has a bad side and everything bad has a good side.*

When you see the bad side in the good, you are oriented towards darkness.

When you see the good side in the bad, you are oriented towards the light.

'What's this now? Can there be positive conditions also that deepen a relationship?' Satyabhama was curious.

'Of course. Let me tell you the story of my own life. I came to know about positive conditions from Narada Muni who told us all these stories that I just narrated to you. In fact, after narrating these three stories he told us the reason why they were about negative conditions. He explained that conditions that benefit only one of the two parties are negative because they are born out of selfishness. While each of these people had valid reasons of their own for making these conditions, they didn't think about the impact of the condition on the other party. They didn't think that they should choose their conditions in consultation with the other person, since it would affect both parties equally.'

 *Positive conditions are like a rainbow that unites the rain with the sun.*

Negative conditions are like lightning that divides even the sky.

'Narada Muni warned us that our odd marriage was at great risk if we didn't adopt the policy of having positive conditions that all of us agreed upon together. He told us the story of Sunda and Upasunda who were the best of friends and in fact brothers. Though they had such an unbreakable bond, the entrance of one woman in their lives ruined their lifelong relationship. The brothers were demonic warriors. They would ransack and loot to gain wealth. They also wanted to become immortal. Thankfully, Lord Brahma wouldn't grant them that boon. They then opted for the next best thing to immortality, which was to choose who would be the one who killed them. Each one chose the other, confident that their love for each other would never wane, at least not to the extent that they would want to kill each other.

'But in walked this beautiful apsara from the heavens named Tillotama, who had been created by Brahma himself to cause conflict between the troublesome brothers. As soon as they set their eyes on the beautiful damsel, they began to fight. Each wanted her for himself. Within moments, they began to assault each other, first verbally, then physically, then brutally and then fatally. That was the end of the relationship and that was the end of the brothers.

'After telling us this story, Narada Muni warned us that our situation was even more dangerous than Sunda and Upasunda's. In our case it was five men and one woman. Naturally, if this marriage had to work, there had to be positive conditions laid down right at the beginning to prevent any strains on the relationship. He explained that positive conditions were simply those conditions that focus on keeping relationships intact. He also said that relationships lasted only on the basis of sacrifice. The more the focus is on exploitation, the more the focus on oneself. The more the focus is on the other, the more the focus on serving. The relationships that focus on purity of purpose are the relationships that survive the test of time.'

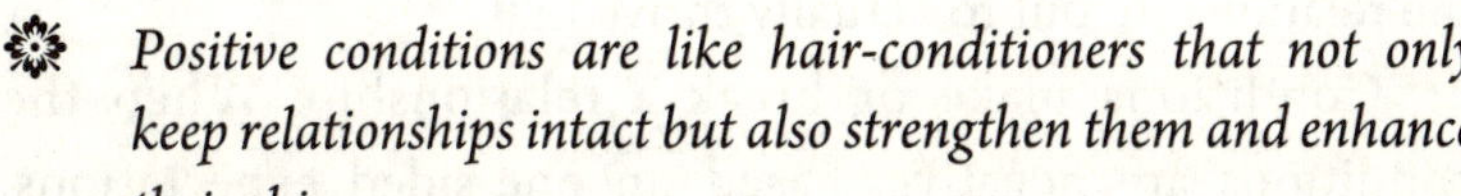

Positive conditions are like hair-conditioners that not only keep relationships intact but also strengthen them and enhance their shine.

'In keeping with his advice my five husbands and I sat together and formulated an agreement. We agreed that at no cost would any of us succumb to individual interests and selfishness. We would not allow the unity between the five brothers and their wife to break. We decided upon four positive conditions. The first was that I would act as the wife to only one of the five Pandava brothers at a time and the time period for each brother would be a year. The second condition was that in the said year none of the other four brothers would come near me or show any kind of affection to me privately or publicly. The others wouldn't even be permitted to enter my private chambers while I was with one of the brothers. The third condition was that if any one of them entered my room while I was with another brother, they would have to go on exile for twelve years. The fourth condition was that after the stipulated period of one year, I would undergo severe austerities and penances to purify myself. Only after that would I spend the next one year with the next brother.

'For so many years we have diligently followed these positive conditions in our relationship and not even once have we experienced friction between us even though the relationship is so odd.'

Satyabhama was deeply affected by Draupadi's story. This final story described the most complicated relationships ever. However, on the strength of the four positive conditions, the Pandavas and Draupadi were managing to not only survive in the relationship but to actually thrive in it.

Conditions make or break a relationship. When the conditions are negative, based on one-sided expectations, selfishness or lack of communication of one's motives, then they strangle a relationship. When conditions are positive, based on mutually beneficial thoughts, selflessness and proper communication of one's intentions, then they help a relationship blossom.

 *Conditions that unite are the conditions that are right.*

CONDITIONS THAT UNITE

Some relationships appear to be genuine and sturdy like cheap imitation products. It feels that they will surely last forever. In fact they manage to convince the whole world that it is going to last forever. Eventually though, like every imitation product, one day the label falls off and the parts start wearing off. You may successfully convince the world that the relationship is real, but the question is, how long will you convince yourself? The difference between genuine and fake is the amount of time it lasts. Genuine relationships 'grow' with time, while fake relationships 'go' with time.

In this assortment of stories, there are several relationships that are examined closely. All seemed genuine at the beginning until they reached a point at which the falseness in some became obvious. In some it took a little longer to establish the falseness. In a relationship, the time between when the first doubt arises and the confirmation of falsity is the most painful one. Undoubtedly, everyone wants to believe that their relationship is an authentic one. However, like Shantanu and Pururava, anyone in an inauthentic relationship has to accept at some point that it's not going to work.

If a condition makes the condition of the relationship better then it's a good condition, but if it worsens the condition of the relationship then it's a bad condition. So, are conditions good or are conditions bad for relationships? Actually nothing in this world is completely good or bad. It all depends on the impact it creates. If anything causes a positive impact in the relationship then it's good and if anything causes a negative impact in a relationship then it's bad. Conditions that unite are the conditions that are right.

Draupadi observed the couples in her husbands' family carefully and studied the trend. She realised that three relationships in the past had not worked out in their family. When she probed further, she surmised that all three had a common cause of disruption. The reason being negative conditions, which were one-sided, with no empathy for the other party. It wasn't simply a lack of empathy but also involved a great deal of selfishness, at least on the part of Urvashi and Satyavati. When Narada Muni told Draupadi and her five husbands that they had to put a few conditions in place to make the relationship work, naturally she panicked. When three relationships in their family had floundered, how would their marriage survive if it was based on conditions? That's when she was enlightened about the positive conditions that unite. When Draupadi and the Pandavas formulated serious positive conditions and followed them strictly, their unconventional relationship not just worked but flourished.

You are loved not so much for what you do but for who you are. Love has to flow steadily like a river. Occasional outbursts do happen in love, just like every river floods occasionally. However, a river is not meant to take but to give. So is love. Unconditional love is about how to give unconditionally. Conditional love is about how to take continuously. One becomes inauthentic in a relationship when one focuses on personal goals and agendas, whilst abandoning collective goals and aspirations.

Urvashi's, Satyavati's and Ganga's love seemed to flow like a river. But the moment the conditions that they had placed were defied, the river flooded their existence. When a river flows gently it nourishes, but when it floods it destroys. When love flows selflessly it nourishes, but when it floods selfishly it destroys.

When selfish conditions surround love, people try to become perfectionists in order to retain that love. Such people convince themselves that in order to experience love, one should be perfect in the eyes of their partner. Perfect here means abiding by the needs, interests and concerns of their partner even at the cost of abandoning their own. Such people repeatedly silence their own voice in order to retain their love. Eventually a time comes when the struggling but failing perfectionist realises that they are loved for what they do and not for who they are. The moment they stop doing what they are expected to do, they stop receiving that conditional love. That realisation marks the beginning of the end of the relationship.

Pururava was ready to do anything to retain Urvashi's love. Shantanu was ready to do anything to retain Ganga's love. They both tried to be the perfect husband and partner. They aligned themselves with the expectations of their wives to perfection. They kept aside their own needs, interests and concerns to focus on their wives'. However, after just one set of questions by Shantanu, Ganga broke off the relationship. After one small mistake by Pururava, Urvashi broke off the relationship. Pururava and Shantanu both realised that their relationships were one-sided. The moment they stopped doing what they were expected to do, they stopped getting the love they were addicted to. That's when they realised that it was an addiction, not love. They realised that they were begging for love and a few pennies of love dropped into a beggar's bowl is no love at all. True love is when you ask for nothing but you get everything.

When requests become demands, love becomes pain. When your conditions are more important than the condition of the person you love, then your love is in a very bad condition. Unconditional love can flow only when unconditional trust is earned. When unconditional trust has to be demanded, conditional love is the result. You may win in enforcing your conditions but you lose in the relationship.

The stories of Shantanu's relationship with Ganga and Satyavati and Pururava's love for Urvashi talk about how negative conditions complicate relationships from the beginning and strangulate them in the end. Draupadi's marriage with the five Pandavas lasted a lifetime, though it was a very awkward configuration, because of Narada Muni's wise advice, given right at the beginning of the relationship. In both sets of stories there were conditions that were applied. However, because there was a fundamental difference in the mindset with which these conditions were applied, the first set of relationships didn't last and left a lifetime of burning scars on both parties. On the other hand, the second set of relationships lasted a lifetime because the conditions were mutually beneficial and positive.

EPILOGUE

After meeting and counselling hundreds of couples for more than a decade, I have realised that there is nothing more important than underlying genuineness to make a relationship last a lifetime. This book is the result of my explorations to help people find that authenticity in those they choose to love.

Each story that I presented has a secret to genuine and lasting love. Though there are six stories, there are only five and a half ways to it. Why not six? Simply because the last way is only half a way. While the other five are clear-cut positive ways, the sixth one has a negative element coupled with a positive one. I recommend considering only the positive element in it and carefully avoiding the negative one.

Each of these keys is simple, yet powerful. Only when you begin to contemplate, assimilate and implement these methods will you understand the power these thoughts have in transforming your relationships.

KEY 1: FORGIVENESS IS KEY

In the beginning of a relationship, it's only the positive side of one another that is visible. As the relationship progresses, the negative side takes prominence causing destabilisation. When the good side is the focus, the bad side is hardly visible. But when the bad side of people you love comes to the forefront, the good side miraculously shrinks or is hardly considered relevant. That is where the role of forgiveness comes in.

The story of Nala and Damayanti is a test of the limits of tolerance and forgiveness. A story of two people who loved each other madly and prioritised each other over everything else. They perceived divine qualities in each other that they couldn't see even in the gods.

Through this story we see the dynamics of what happens when people who have such strong bonds come across weaknesses and flaws in each other. A relationship reaches the brink of destruction due to the bad behaviour of one partner but is brought back to its original healthy state due to the tolerance and forgiveness of the other partner. Tolerate first and forgive next. It's not enough to tolerate the weaknesses of people we love; it is more important to forgive them.

Forgiveness is the first key to make a relationship last for a lifetime.

KEY 2: APPRECIATIVE EXPRESSIONS OF LOVE

Love is a very important element of life. Expressing that love is even more crucial. Relationships begin with expressions that touch the heart. But, over time, the relationship plateaus and one tends to forget this fact.

The story of Rukmini explores the power of words in relationships. The world knows Krishna to be a master of words but this story describes Rukmini's mastery over the world of words. The story begins with Rukmini taking the step of expressing her love through a letter.

When words are woven in an intricate, loving way, they permanently embroider the design of love in the fabric of our heart. Thus Rukmini's words affected Krishna. He decided to drop everything to reciprocate her love.

Your vocabulary is not formed with words but with intentions. The feeling of being loveable is something that no gift can replace. People need a daily quota of loving words to gently remind them that they are loveable.

Appreciative expressions of love is the second key to make a relationship last for a lifetime.

KEY 3: TRUSTING RELATIONSHIPS

Trust is the foundation on which relationships thrive. Without trust they only strive.

The story of Shakuntala and Dushyanta is a story of trust. This tale explores a seldom-discussed aspect that is nevertheless very important for lasting relationships, especially when there is doubt created due to circumstances. It's a story in which two people allow their inner voices to guide them into trusting one another even in the midst of the greatest storm of doubt.

When Shakuntala learns to trust herself, she ends up learning to trust Dushyanta as well. Trust in others begins by trusting oneself first, the inner voice, second and life itself, third. There may be many reasons to lose trust in oneself, in one's inner voice as well as in life. But there is one very good reason to keep trusting all over again, and that is the possibility of experiencing lasting love.

Trust is the third key to make a relationship last for a life time.

KEY 4: GOOD TIMES HELP TIDE OVER BAD TIMES

Time is the world's most expensive currency. When you invest time, it means that you are investing your most expensive currency in that person. Probably the best way to understand your priorities is to monitor the way you spend the currency of time.

This key explores the story of two couples who invest time in each other. Though it may seem to be a small detail in the two intertwined stories, it is really the essence of the stories. Udayana and Vasavadatta as well as Lohajanga and Rupinika build their relationships based on quality time spent in each other's company.

Alignment is important for relationships to last. Alignment is about sitting in the same vehicle, facing the same direction and moving towards the same destination. To align with one another, two people need to have deep, meaningful, soul-searching conversations with each other. These conversations are about revealing one's thoughts, feelings and fears without inhibitions and with utter honesty.

Spending quality and quantity time is the fourth key to make a relationship last for a lifetime.

KEY 5: THE DETERMINATION TO STAY TOGETHER

Determination means doing what's necessary even when it seems difficult. Determination allows us to act even when we don't know how to. The mind automatically generates internal resources that are needed to overcome resistance, setbacks and self-doubt, given enough determination and will.

This key explores the story of Satyavan and Savitri who loved each other more than anything else in the world. Savitri was resolute not to let go of the relationship even in the face of death itself.

Those who are determined to commit themselves to a relationship for life understand that if someone is not satisfied with one person, they will never be satisfied with anyone. The determination to stick to one relationship actually increases the overall levels of happiness and contentment in a human being.

Determination to stay in a relationship is the fifth key to make a relationship last for a lifetime.

KEY 5.5: CONDITIONS THAT UNITE

Conditions can either better the condition of a relationship or worsen it. So are conditions good or are conditions bad for relationships? Actually nothing in this world is purely good or bad. It all depends on the impact it creates. If anything causes a positive impact on a relationship, then it is good and if anything causes a negative impact on a relationship, then it is bad. Conditions that unite are conditions that are right.

The stories of Shantanu's relationship with Ganga and Satyavati and Pururava's love for Urvashi talk about how negative conditions complicate relationships from the beginning and strangulate them in the end. Whereas Draupadi's marriage with the five Pandavas lasted a lifetime. Though it was a very awkward configuration, Narada Muni's wise advice given right at the start of the relationship helped them draw out positive conditions.

In both sets of stories conditions were applied. However, because there was a fundamental difference in the mindset with which these conditions were implemented, the first set of relationships didn't last and left a lifetime of burning scars. On the other hand, the second set of relationships lasted because the conditions were mutually beneficial and positive.

Half of this key is about how negative conditions don't work in a relationship. The other half is about how positive conditions preserve one. A positive condition is the last half-key to make a relationship last for a lifetime.

If you are reading this, I assume that you have completed reading the book. Hopefully these love stories have touched your heart, the adventures have exhilarated your mind and the knowledge in them has inspired your intellect. Now it's time for action! Here are some thoughts that can help you make the most of this book.

First and foremost, I would like you to spend a little more time on understanding the stories and the connections between the stories and the keys for lasting relationships embedded within them. Carefully go through the short lessons inside and the summary lesson after the chapters.

Secondly, make a note of the most powerful points in each chapter and contemplate upon them. Thirdly, create a set of action points to implement each key in your own life on the most important relationship that you cherish. Fourthly, don't just make points on paper, make it a point to implement them in action. Lastly, observe what works and what doesn't work for you.

It may seem intimidating at first to make this effort, but begin with a small step. I would like to offer you my help in the process of implementing these keys in discovering the joys of genuine, lasting relationships. Please feel free to connect with me and share your experiences, either of reading this book or of implementing these ideas in your relationships. I wish you good times ahead, basking in loving relationships and self-growth. Stay in touch…